By

Keith Wolfe

Cadmus Publishing
CadmusPublishing.com

BETRAYED

DISCLAIMER:
The thoughts, opinions, and expressions herein are those of the author and do not reflect those of Cadmus Publishing LLC. Any similarities to actual events or people are purely coincidental. Names and distinguishing characteristics may have been changed to preserve the identities of any individuals. Published by Cadmus Publishing LLC. P. O. Box 8664. Haledon, NJ 07538

Web: Cadmuspublishing.com
Web: Booksbyprisoners.com
Web: MusicbyPrisoners.com
Facebook.com/Cadmuspublishing
Business email: admin@cadmuspublishing.com
Author email: info@cadmuspublishing.com
Phone: 360.565.6459

ISBN # 978-1-63751-489-4
Book Catalog Info Categories:
Fiction/Suspense/Thriller

CadmusPublishing.com

PROLOGUE

She screamed.

No one heard her because she was alone in the old, two-story white house where a single bare bulb burned. A failing streetlight buzzed outside on the hot, humid night that was about to become stormy.

Elizabeth screamed again, trying to make the baby come out, pushing, pushing, screaming, screaming louder. Lightning flashed as the child's head appeared. One. More. Push! and the child slipped onto the bed with no one to catch her. The young mother picked up her infant, and a faint cry came from the tiny girl. The baby cried again, and a rumble of thunder echoed across the tiny neighborhood.

The mother put the child to her breast and felt the colostrum let down. Elizabeth was ready to nurse this child, to take care of her, even if no one else would stand up to help. Lightning flashed, much closer now, and Elizabeth counted: two eyes, two ears, ten fingers, ten toes.

"You're perfect!" she said to her daughter. "Now, what should I name you?"

Lightning. "I'll name you Grace." Thunder, quick, loud, intense, close. "Amazing Grace." She leaned back and let the baby nurse.

"This world is tough and evil, Grace," she said after a moment, "but we'll be tougher. Don't trust those bastards out there."

Grace nursed. Elizabeth smiled.

CHAPTER ONE

There weren't many neighbors near the old white house, and after a few years, they stopped chattering about the single woman and her little girl whom no one ever seemed to see. When the school people came to visit, Elizabeth curtly told them she would homeschool Grace, and would they please mind their liberal government-school business. They went away. She didn't answer the door for the Mormon missionaries and the Jehovah's Witnesses who knocked. No one else ever came to the door.

When Grace was thirteen, Elizabeth decided it was time to put her on the school bus and let her little girl learn some of the hard things. Elizabeth knew that she didn't understand geometry or chemistry or economics. But she knew lies when she heard them. She knew dangerous things when she saw them, so Elizabeth would quiz her daughter every night to ensure what she was being taught.

Grace was skinny, beanpole skinny, with long, blonde hair that came to her waist. Her eyes were intensely blue, but people seldom saw that. She kept her gaze downward. She hid her face behind her hair. Grace always wore old-fashioned dresses that covered her from neck to ankles. The kids at Wolf County High

School never really noticed her, and that was fine with Grace and Elizabeth. But that wouldn't last.

Nacole was bright, fun, vivacious, captain of the Wolf County cheerleading squad, with a smile that could light up the darkest night, and she loved everybody. But as the last day of the senior year approached, Nacole realized she had missed someone. Nacole walked past the overstuffed wood-and-glass trophy case on her way to her locker, to clean it out one final time. Then, she spotted Grace.

That weird, skinny, blonde girl with long hair also cleaning out her locker. What was her name . . . Grace? She didn't know anything about Grace and had never introduced herself to the lean blonde girl, and it was time to change that.

"Hey, Grace! How've you been?" Nacole asked.

Grace froze, unsure of how to respond. No one ever talked to her.

"Hey, I'm talking to you, silly!" Nacole said with a little laugh, amused at how flabbergasted the other girl was.

"Uh, hi, Nacole," Grace finally squeaked after opening and closing her mouth a few times.

"Are you excited about graduation tonight?" Nacole continued, not noticing the other girl's discomfort or perhaps ignoring it. "What are you going to do after you graduate?"

2

Grace tucked her hair behind her ears and stood up straight. "Um, I don't think I'm coming to graduation. My mom doesn't want to come . . . and I don't know what I'm going to do after graduation. I haven't talked it over with Mom yet. I'm sure she has something planned for me."

Nacole frowned. She looked confused. "Why doesn't your mom want to come to your graduation?"

"Mom has had the say-so on everything I've ever done since I was born. I've been shut up in that old house of ours my whole life."

She looked Nacole right in the eye, and Nacole saw, for the first time, the intense blue of Grace's eyes.

Nacole shuddered a little as Grace continued.

"I'm eighteen now, and I'm done playing Mom's stupid little games. It's like, 'Come straight home, Grace, don't talk to anyone, Grace, everyone's evil, Grace.' I'm beginning to think that she's the evil one."

Tears began to run down her face. Nacole put her arms around her and began to pat her on the back. Grace pulled away.

"I'm so sorry," Grace said. "I didn't mean to vent on you."

"It's OK," Nacole said.

"Mom never leaves the house," Grace said. "If she needs something, she sends me after it, always after dark, and I . . . I get scared walking around town at night all by myself. But if I don't go, she'll lock me in the basement and turn the light out."

Tears continued running down onto her plain, long dress.

"Oh, my God, Grace," Nacole said. "I'm so sorry. No one ever knew." Her own tears were falling now, and she turned away so her new friend couldn't see. "I . . . I wasn't expecting that." She wiped her cheek, trying to be careful not to smear her carefully applied mascara.

"So . . . what made your mom like that?" Nacole asked. "Something had to make her like this."

Grace shook her head. "I don't know. She's been that way ever since I can remember. From what I can gather, she must have had a really bad relationship with some guy when she was younger, and I am the byproduct of it."

"But I don't know who my father is," Grace continued. "If I ask, Mom just gets pissed off, so I don't ask anymore."

Nacole just shook her head and sniffled a little.

"You know, Grace, you could come to graduation anyway . . . I'll make sure the cheerleaders and my friends all cheer when you walk," Nacole said, smiling. Grace just looked at her shoes, and a tear fell on the floor.

"I . . . I . . . can't," she sobbed. "Mom would beat the hell out of me for defying her."

Nacole looked thoughtful. Then she gave Grace another smile.

"I've got a plan," she said. "Graduation starts at seven, right? It'll take a couple of hours, and by the time all the hugs and picture-taking gets done, it'll be, like, ten o'clock, and dark, right?"

Grace nodded. She wasn't sure where this was going.

"We're going to have a party by the lake," Nacole said. "Now, what time does your mom go to bed?"

Grace thought. "Oh, about nine-thirty, ten o'clock. She doesn't stay up late. Leaving the lights on costs too much, she says. But Mom will beat me if she knew I went to a party."

Nacole gave Grace her best smile yet, the kind that lights up a room. "What she doesn't know won't hurt you."

Grace almost smiled this time. It felt strange. She never smiled.

"Besides, you just said you weren't going to let your mom ruin your life anymore, right?"

"I did say that, didn't I?" Grace wondered about it for a minute. "But it's a long way to the lake. How would I get there in the dark?"

"In Kent's car, silly," Nacole replied. "I'll be there with Kent, my boyfriend, and the car he got for graduation. We'll be waiting at the bottom of the hill by your house at ten-thirty. Make sure your eighteen-year-old, freedom-loving ass is ready, girl!"

The plain girl and the cheer captain hugged, hard.

"Yes!" Grace said. "Yes, yes, yes!" If she'd ever danced, she would have danced now, but she didn't know how to dance.

"Oh, Grace," Nacole said. "Make sure you bring something to swim in."

That stopped Grace cold. "I can't swim," she said. "I've never been swimming." She looked down at her shoes again. "I'm sorry, Nacole. Let's forget the whole thing. I'll just ruin your night."

Nacole stared at Grace with mock sternness. "No one is going to ruin my graduation night," she said, pointing a finger at Grace, "unless they don't show up. Got that, girlfriend?"

Nacole's hand went up in a high-five. Grace shrank back a little from the raised hand. "Grace! High-five! Slap my hand, girl!"

Grace did as she was told, and suddenly, she got it. The two girls hugged again.

"I better get home," Grace said. "I can't be late."

"So . . . 10:30, bottom of the hill."

Grace slammed the rest of her stuff from her locker into her backpack and ran out the door, catching the school bus just before the door closed. She breathed deeply, looked around, and realized she was the only senior on board. When she got to the old white house, she opened the door and tried to stay calm.

"Where have you been?" Elizabeth growled.

"I cleaned out my locker, Mama. The school bus ran a little late because everyone was packing up their stuff. It's the last day of school."

Elizabeth grabbed a Marlboro Red from the pack on the table next to her recliner. She didn't bother to turn down the volume on the big-screen TV.

"Did you talk to anyone today?" Elizabeth demanded.

Grace was used to the grilling, as it happened every day. "It was just another boring day at school," Grace responded. "But there was this one girl who tried to talk to me. She asked if I would be coming to graduation tonight. I told her no."

Elizabeth looked at Grace furiously. "What's that little bitch's name? Do you know? Did she tell you?"

"Her name is Nacole Stafford, Mama," Grace said. "Everyone knows who she is. She's the most popular girl in school."

Elizabeth crushed her cigarette and lit up another one with a vengeance. "Don't ever talk to that little slut again, you hear me? Don't even look in her direction." Elizabeth took a long drag on her

Marlboro and blew out the smoke. "I knew her daddy in high school. He's a piece of shit. All them people are evil!"

"They don't seem evil to me, Mama."

"How would you know?" Elizabeth snapped. "You ain't been around them people like I have."

"Mama, I'm around those people every day at school. I see 'em. I see how they are."

Elizabeth struggled to sit up in her recliner. She looked straight at her daughter. "That's different. Just stay as far away from 'em as you can. Don't talk to none of 'em." She glanced away for an instant. "That's where I made my mistakes, becoming friends with them rich assholes!"

"What'd they do to you, Mama?" Grace asked. "Why do you hate them so bad?"

Elizabeth turned away. "I just hope when I'm gone that you'll stay as far away from them as you can. Don't let 'em hurt you like they hurt me."

Grace stalked over to the recliner and stood between her mother and the TV. Grace started to cry. "Mama, tell me, what did they do to you? Dammit, I'm your daughter. I deserve to know!"

Elizabeth's face turned bright red. She struggled to her feet and stood face-to-face with the gangly teenager.

"You need to get your little ass up them stairs," Elizabeth shouted, "and get out of them school clothes before you really piss me off!"

Grace was shaking, but she stood her ground.

"Why can't you just tell me the truth, Mama?" Grace sobbed. She took a ragged breath and looked Elizabeth in the eye. "Who's my father?" she demanded.

Elizabeth's fists tightened. She took a step closer to her daughter.

"This is bullshit, Mama," Grace continued. "I'm eighteen now. I deserve to know."

Elizabeth turned and stomped to the kitchen. Grace watched her mother go but didn't follow. Instead, she walked up the stairs, then slammed her bedroom door so hard the windows in the old house shook. Grace locked it, even though that was against Mama's rules. The young woman curled up on her bed, crying silently.

"Why?" she thought. "Why won't she tell me the truth about what happened? Who is my father? Why all the secrets?"

Grace realized she must have fallen asleep for a bit as she sat up and saw that she was still in her school clothes. She changed, blew her nose, unlocked the door, and came down the stairs quietly.

A cloud of smoke hovered over the recliner, and the TV channels kept changing every few seconds. Almost normal, Grace thought.

"Have you been crying?" Elizabeth asked, without taking her eyes off the TV.

"No, Mama," Grace lied. "I just have a headache."

"So you're not mad that I won't let you go to graduation, are you, baby?"

Grace rubbed her temples. Now she really was getting a headache. "No, Mama. Too many people there, and I don't like the crowds . . ."

Grace wasn't sure if it even sounded like the truth.

"That's good, baby," Elizabeth smiled. "I'm proud of you."

Elizabeth finally settled the channel on some talking heads squawking about the latest outrage in Washington.

"Them people are all evil out there, Grace," Elizabeth said, "especially boys. They'll break your heart and walk away laughing."

"I know, Mama," Grace sighed. "You've told me that a thousand times, but you've never told me why."

"And I'm gonna tell you a thousand times more, baby, 'til it sticks in your scrawny little head and you stop asking questions. Time will come when you'll see who they really are. They're just a bunch of rich-ass people that only give a shit about themselves and nobody else."

Grace shook her head. Not for the first time, she thought her mother really was crazy.

"Well, Mama, I'm going back upstairs to read, OK?"

"Sure, baby. Supper will be on the table in a while."

"Let me know when it's ready, Mama."

Grace went upstairs, looked at the clock on her dresser, and picked up the book on her nightstand. She lay down, started reading, but didn't get far before sleep overtook her again.

She awoke with a start. It was almost dark outside.

Grace ran downstairs. Her mother was still in the recliner in front of the TV.

"Why didn't you call me for supper?" Grace wondered. She could feel a little irritation sneaking into her voice.

"I did, baby, but you were fast asleep. You said you had a headache, so I just let you sleep. Your food's still on the stove. Grab yourself a plate and come sit with your mama."

Grace did just that. She came back and sat on the couch, picking at her food. She looked at the clock—it was almost ten. How was she going to get back upstairs and get ready for the party?

She took a few more bites. "I'm going back to bed, Mama. I'm sure I'll feel better in the morning. Good night."

"Good night," Elizabeth answered. "Rinse off your plate and put it in the sink."

Grace locked the door, for the second time today, the second time in her life. She liked the sound of it. And she realized she had nothing to wear. She began rummaging through her closet of other people's castoffs, finally settling on her shortest skirt and a bright yellow blouse.

"This will have to do," she said to herself. She ran a brush through her long, blonde hair, then pulled it back into a ponytail. She looked again in the mirror. "I wish I had some makeup," she thought, then began pinching her own cheeks to get some color into her pale skin.

Outside the door, she heard the stairs creak under her mother's weight, the old wood cracking and popping with every slow step. She heard her mother shuffle down the hall to her room, and heard the door close. Grace heaved a sigh of relief. At least Mama wasn't going to sleep in the recliner tonight, like she sometimes did.

Headlights reflected off her bedroom wall. "Right on time," Grace said. "That's got to be Nacole and her boy."

Grace pulled the curtains apart and saw a car parked down the hill. She popped the window locks, then slowly raised the sash, trying not to make a sound. She threw one leg, then the other out the window, stepping onto the steep roof. She edged over to where an old oak tree had grown right up against the house. "Someday, that tree is going to come down and take the house with it," she thought, "but I'm glad it's there now." She climbed into the tree, climbed down to the lowest limb, then hung on and let go. She hit the ground.

Grace had sneaked in and out of the house dozens of times when she was little, going out at all hours of the night, looking up at the stars in the sky, imagining that she was a normal girl with a normal family.

The headlights flashed and brought her back to reality. Grace took off toward the car, and she saw Nacole standing on the hood.

"You're here!" Grace shouted.

Nacole jumped down from the car and ran toward her newest friend.

"Of course we're here!" Nacole said as Grace leaped into Nacole's arms. "I was worried about you!"

"I wouldn't miss this for the world," Grace gasped, out of breath from the run down the hill. She climbed into the backseat as Kent started the car.

"This is going to sound crazy," Grace said, "but I've never ridden in a car before. I've ridden the school bus, but I've never been in anybody's car."

"Well, I hope you like my car," Kent said from the front seat. "I'm Kent. Nacole's told me all about you, Grace." Kent was tall, blonde, and stocky. "We're going to have a great time tonight!"

"I'm ready," Grace said. "I gotta ask. Is there going to be booze there?"

Kent laughed. "What kind do you like?" he asked.

"I don't know. I've never drunk before. I mean, what does it taste like?"

"Some of it tastes like shit," Nacole laughed. "But don't worry, I'll make sure to get you stuff you'll like. Just trust me."

"Ah, most people just drink to get drunk," Kent said.

"Really?" Grace said. "Maybe I better get started."

"How do you like live music?" Kent asked.

"You mean like a band playing just for us? Like on TV, only in real life?" Grace had to think about that for a while.

"You're in for a treat, Grace," Kent said. "The band we got is called Hill Street Lunatic. They're from the state capital, but they play a lot around here. They're really good!"

"Lots of kids are bringing their jet skis," Nacole added. "And you're gonna love the giant bonfire!"

Grace's eyes widened as Kent pulled into the parking lot by the lake. The bonfire was already going, lighting up the night. She heard music like she'd never heard before. People were dancing and shouting and running. Grace got out of the car and just looked, just drank in the scene.

"That's . . . one . . . big-ass bonfire," she finally said.

"It sure is," Kent agreed, smiling. "Wanna go for a ride on a jet ski?"

"What's that?" Grace wondered aloud. Nacole pointed to the personal watercraft buzzing around out on the lake.

"Those things. They're a blast!"

Grace shuddered and kind of shrank back into herself. "I . . . I'd be too scared. I can't swim, and being in the dark . . . well, I start to panic. Maybe it's from all the times Mama locked me up in the basement in the dark."

"Yeah . . . maybe. I'm so sorry, Grace," Nacole said.

"That's OK," Grace said. "I'm eighteen, and I'm going to do what I want."

"Good for you, girl," Nacole said. "Let's go find us some booze!"

The two girls took off for the beach, laughing. "Look at that! They've got a real bar set up!"

The two ran toward the open-front tent with a bar set up in the opening. The scene was lit by tiki torches.

"Oh, my gosh, Jimmy!" Nacole squealed. "They got you working the bar tonight? Boy, you got screwed!"

"Go ahead and laugh, Nacole," said the freshly graduated teen behind the bar. "They just put me, the best-looking guy ever to attend Wolf County High School, behind the bar because they're all jealous. If I were out there with my game on, I'd take all the girls home with me."

"Oh, you wish!" Nacole shot back.

"Besides, my Uncle Guido owns this setup—you know, the uncle who's got the beer distributorship and the liquor warehouse?"

Jimmy smiled. "Party's on him tonight. But there's the tip jar, ladies," he added, pointing to the gallon jar already a quarter-full of bills and change. "Nacole, who's the hottie with you? Have I seen her before?"

"You might have seen her around school, Jimmy. This is Grace. She's in our class, but she's pretty shy."

"Oh, yeah," Jimmy said. "They called your name tonight, but no one was there, and I was wondering, who's that? Now I know," he continued with his shark-like smile and put two wine coolers on the bar. Nacole stuck out her tongue at him playfully and stuffed a couple of bills into the tip jar.

"Tell Uncle Guido we love him," Nacole said.

"This is fantastic," Grace said as she took a big swig of the sugary alcoholic drink. "What do you call this?"

"That's a wine cooler," Nacole replied.

"And I've got lots more in my basement for after the party. You girls are invited," Jimmy shared, his smile never changing.

"You know I've got a boyfriend," Nacole said.

"Yeah, Kent's a lucky guy, for sure." He paused a beat. "So you're gonna come to my house? It's graduation night, ladies, a time of change and new beginnings and all that."

"In your dreams, Romeo," Nacole said. "But thanks for the wine coolers."

Grace just kept swigging down her wine cooler.

"I think he's kind of cute," Grace said to Nacole. "Where's he live?"

"Whoa, slow down, girl," Nacole warned her. "You're drinking that wine way too fast, and you don't know what kind of trouble you might find yourself in. You've never drunk before, and you don't know how to handle it. It's gonna set you on your ass."

"Huh?" Grace said as she finished the bottle.

"You're going to get really drunk and stupid, Grace," Nacole said. "Slow down."

Grace just smiled. The alcohol hadn't really hit yet.

"Look, Grace, there's my best friend Becky," Nacole said. "Let's go talk to her."

Becky was pulling on a wine cooler of her own. "Hey, Nacole, who's the girl tagging along with you like a puppy dog?" Becky looked Grace up and down as if she were something nasty.

"Becky, she graduated with us," Nacole said.

"Oh, yeah, you're . . . whaddyacallit . . . Grace, right? You don't talk much. What are you, like, retarded?"

Grace looked at the ground. "No, I just don't like talking to people I don't know."

Becky took another swig. "So, you gonna swim? Gonna go out on a jet ski?"

"I don't know how to swim," Grace said.

"Then what did you come here for if you ain't gonna do nothing?"

"Grace, come on," Nacole said, giving Becky a mean look as she turned to walk away.

"Listen, Nacole, if you'd rather I just left so you can hang around with Becky . . ."

"Forget it, Grace," Nacole answered, putting her arm around Grace. "Sometimes that girl can be such a bitch. I think she's pissed off that you're hanging with me, and I'm not hanging with her."

"Well, Nacole, I promise I wouldn't mind . . ."

"Look, would you like to spend your whole graduation night with that bitch?" Nacole asked. "Me neither." She laughed.

"More wine coolers?" Grace said brightly.

"You got it, girl," Nacole said as they made their way back to Jimmy's bar on the beach.

"Hey, Jimmy, two more wine coolers," Grace said, a little louder than she expected.

"I knew you girls would come back to me," Jimmy smiled. "You guys missed me, didn't you?"

"Yes, I missed you," Grace said, looking Jimmy right in the eye and smiling. "I've only had one drink, Jimmy. Can you fix that?"

Jimmy looked at Nacole. She shook her head, smiled, then nodded.

"She's never been drunk before," Nacole said. "I don't think it'll take very much."

Jimmy nodded wisely as he popped the tops off two more wine coolers. "Uncle Guido never lets the liquor run out," Jimmy said. "Party on, girls!"

Elizabeth tossed and turned in her bed, trying to get to sleep, but worried about her little girl who had gone to bed not feeling well. Truth be told, she was feeling a little guilty as well. She struggled to sit up, felt around for a smoke, lit it, then slipped into her bedroom slippers.

She slipped down the hall to her daughter's room and knocked gently on the door. "Hey, baby, you OK?" she asked. No answer.

Elizabeth tapped again, a little harder. "Baby, are you all right?" she asked a little louder. Nothing.

Elizabeth tried the doorknob, and to her surprise, it was locked. *Locked?* she thought. *She's not allowed to lock her door. I'm the only one who can lock doors in this house.*

"Baby?" she shouted, beating on the bedroom door with her fists. "Open the door! Open the damn door!" Elizabeth hit the door as hard as she could. She was near tears. Grace would pay for this.

Elizabeth took a deep breath and stepped back from the door. "I bet she snuck out the window," she said to herself. "Defiant little wench. She won't get away with this."

She climbed down the stairs, put on her shoes, and began walking down the road toward the corner store where she'd sent Grace for all those years. It had been a long time since she'd been there herself, but it hadn't changed much. At the cash register, a teenage couple was buying chips, soda, and candy. Elizabeth walked up to them.

"Do either of you know a girl named Grace Nelson?" she asked. "Skinny, long blonde hair. She graduated today."

The guy looked at the girl and shook his head.

"No, ma'am," he replied. The girl shook her head. "I might have heard the name around school, but I don't know who she is."

"So where you going with that stuff?" Elizabeth asked innocently. "Got a party tonight? Don't worry; I won't say anything."

"Yes, ma'am," the boy said again. "A big one. Big graduation party down at the lake."

Elizabeth's expression didn't change, but she thought, *Gotcha. You can't hide from your mama.* She smiled at the couple. "Any way you guys could give me a ride over to the lake? My daughter is sickly, and in her rush to go she forgot her medicine."

Why sure, ma'am," the girl said. "That's where we're going, and everybody's invited."

"Hey, Jimmy, hand us a couple of beach towels for us to sit on," Nacole said. "We're going to go sit on the beach."

Jimmy pulled a couple of beach towels emblazoned with his uncle's beer brand off a shelf and handed them to the girls. "Have fun, ladies," he said.

"Come on, Grace," Nacole said excitedly. "Let's go down to the water and sit down before we both fall down." Both girls laughed.

"Oh, my gosh," Grace said. "This is the best time of my life. I will remember this until the day I die."

"I'm so glad you're having fun," Nacole said. "It makes me so happy to hear that."

Both girls lay back on their beach towels and looked up at the stars. After a while, Nacole looked around to see what everyone else was doing, and there she was: Becky, staring at her with angry eyes. Nacole turned away and looked out at the water.

"Anybody know where Kent's at?" It was Becky, shouting loudly.

"I'm over here, by the fire," Kent called out. Becky waved him over, and he took off running toward her.

"So, what's up with Nacole?" Becky asked Kent once he arrived. "She's totally ignored me all night, and it's starting to piss me off."

22

"Oh, you know Nacole," Kent said. "Always picking up strays. She's trying to help out Grace. You know, that kid's had a really tough life. Her mother's abused her and wouldn't even let her walk for graduation. Grace had to sneak out of her house just to be here."

"I guess . . ." Becky paused for a second. "I guess I'm not mad. I did talk to both of them a little while ago."

"Oh, really?" Kent asked.

"Yeah, Grace seems OK," Becky said. "I guess she's cool."

"I really thought so, too," Kent agreed.

"So why don't you give Grace a ride on your Jet Ski? She doesn't look like she's having much fun just lying there. She told me she wanted you to take her out to the middle of the lake."

"Really?" Kent asked, always up for an adventure. "I'll go and ask her."

"Hey, Kent," Grace said as he walked up. She was slurring her words a little. "Hey, Kent! You ever look at the stars when you're drunk? They move one way, and my head moves the other, and it's so messed up." She started giggling. So did Nacole. Kent started laughing, too.

"So, I hear you want to take a ride on my Jet Ski," Kent finally said.

"Oh, hell no," Grace responded. "I don't know how to swim. No friggin' way am I gettin' on that thing."

Kent laughed. He figured she was just kidding. "Grace, you don't need to know how to swim. Your feet never touch the water, and I'll make sure you wear a life jacket. You'll be fine."

"Really?" Grace said reluctantly. Her eyes were having trouble focusing.

"Really," Kent said. "And I'll take it slow." Grace looked pleadingly at Nacole.

"Go ahead, Grace," Nacole said. "Put on the life jacket. You'll have fun, I promise!"

Grace still felt a little reservation, but the alcohol was making it hard to remember why. Finally, she said, "Why not? Let's go!"

She stood up quickly, and suddenly Kent and Nacole found their arms full of girl. "Whoa . . . what happened? The ground fell out from under me," Grace slurred. With Kent on one side and Nacole on the other, Grace stumbled to where the Jet Ski was parked on the sand.

"Maybe I shouldn't be doing this . . ." Grace mumbled. Kent pulled out an orange life jacket from underneath the watercraft's seat and put it over Grace's head. He expertly tied the straps on the life jacket, pulling them tight around the skinny girl's body. Even so, it felt loose, but Kent knew he'd be going slow. He climbed onto the machine and patted the seat behind him.

"Climb on, Grace, and put your arms around me," Kent said to her confidently. Grace looked confused and looked at Nacole for assurance. Nacole nodded and winked, letting Grace know that everything was OK.

"I'll go slow. You'll be fine." He started the Jet Ski's engine and pulled out into the lake. Grace looked back at Nacole, her face white as a sheet. She was hanging on to Kent with a death grip.

"Have fun, Grace!" Nacole shouted over the engine noise. She added something else, but Grace couldn't hear it as Kent revved the engine and the machine drove down the shoreline. The wind hit Grace, and suddenly her fear fell away, at least a little.

"This is kind of awesome," she shouted into Kent's ear. She didn't loosen her grip on him in the least. He opened the throttle a little more, and Grace's long hair streamed behind her. He took a long turn and headed back to the beach, but Nacole waved him away, telling Kent to take her along for a longer ride. Kent steered the watercraft along the shore of the lake.

Grace's head was spinning, and not just from the wine coolers. She was snuggled up against Kent's body, and the smell of his sweat and tanning lotion was intoxicating. She took the time to think about the firm feel of his abs, the way he controlled the machine under them, the wind, the night . . . Grace had never felt like this before, ever, and she wondered if she'd ever feel like this again.

Kent turned around and yelled, "You OK back there?"

Grace, actually touching a boy's body, looked into Kent's eyes, letting him know she was fine and approved of the experience. Man, she really approved. He turned back to the water, and she closed her eyes, just feeling, just smelling the sweat and the water as she wished the life jacket wasn't in the way, but she got close enough to put her head on his shoulder. She just rode, it seemed like forever . . . until the engine stopped.

Grace opened her eyes, expecting to be back on the beach. But she wasn't. There was nothing but darkness and water and silence around the two of them.

"Um . . . where are we?" Grace asked, feeling the panic of years of her mother's warnings coming out.

"Out in the middle of the lake," Kent said nonchalantly. "It's so calm, so peaceful. Oh, look—the moon's coming up! I wanted to surprise you."

Grace started to breathe heavily. This was all too fast, too much, too soon.

"No, no, no, no!" Grace stammered. "You have to take me back! I'm scared."

"Nothing to be scared about," Kent answered. "I'm right here with you."

Grace started to cry. "Please take me back to the beach. I have to go. Please, please, please!" She started to hyperventilate.

"Calm down, Grace. Please calm down." Kent tried to sound firm and in control, but didn't quite succeed. "Stay in your seat, or you'll turn us over."

"I . . . I . . . I can't breathe," Grace gasped. "Take me back now. I can't . . . breathe!"

Kent started the engine. He had heard enough.

"Kent!!!" Grace screamed.

Back on the beach, Nacole saw a group of teenagers gathering to look out on the water and started pointing and laughing. She heard Grace's panicked cries out on the lake. And then she saw Becky and knew something was going horribly wrong.

"The little retard is scared of the water, isn't she?" Becky smiled. "And she's probably scared of the dark, too. And I bet she can't swim. How pathetic."

"You . . . bitch," Nacole said. "You better hope nothing happens to her."

"Or what?" Becky shot back. "I'm supposed to be your best friend. You've hardly spoken one word to me all night on the most important day of our lives. You've totally ignored me this whole night. So I figured I'd find a way to get your attention. Pretty good, right?"

"You know what? You're one greedy bitch," Nacole shouted. "I was just trying to give Grace one good night out, so when she goes back home to all the bullshit she lives with, she'll have at least one great memory of high school. You've never wanted for anything, and Grace never has had anything."

Out on the water, Kent throttled up the Jet Ski and headed for shore. Suddenly, he felt Grace's arms let go of him. He turned around. She was gone.

She was gone. It took a second to sink in, but Grace was gone!

Kent throttled way back and turned the Jet Ski as hard as he could. He looked in the wake. He looked on both sides, but he saw nothing. The rising moon lit the surface of the lake, with the light scattering off the waves caused by the watercraft.

But there was no Grace. He cut the motor. He listened. The only sound was the water lapping against the Jet Ski's hull.

"Grace!" he shouted. "Grace! Answer me!"

Nothing.

"Grace! Grace! Where are you?!"

A flash of lightning lit up the sky. Kent looked up. There were no clouds, not yet, but a flash like that had to mean a big storm was on the way. Kent was really getting scared.

Another flash of lightning, more intense, split the night. Kent looked and saw—could it be? . . . fog? How? This fog was thicker than he'd ever seen, and it rolled rapidly across the surface of the lake toward Kent. He started the Jet Ski and raced, full throttle, toward the beach.

Nacole saw Kent's Jet Ski racing in, and he hit the beach going full speed, running up the sand. *That's unusual,* Nacole thought.

"Nacole! Nacole!" he shouted. "Grace is gone! She's out there somewhere! We need help!"

"What?" Nacole was out of breath as she ran up to Kent's watercraft. "What do you mean, Grace is gone? Where is she?"

"I don't know, Nacole." Kent was starting to panic. "She started to go crazy on me. She said she couldn't breathe, so I started back to shore as fast as I could. Then I felt her let go. She had to fall off into the water or something, because when I looked back I couldn't find her anywhere. No screaming. No splashing. Nothing. I came back in to get some help!"

"Yeah, we need to get back out there," Nacole agreed.

"But there's a big thunderstorm coming or something," Kent said, catching his breath. "And look at that fog bank out there. That's the thickest fog I've ever seen."

Becky ran up to the two on the beach. Before she could say a word, Nacole turned toward the girl who had once been her best friend and let her have it.

"Look what you've done!" Nacole grabbed Becky by the throat. "You killed her!" Kent stepped up and pulled the two girls apart.

"I'm sorry! I'm so sorry!" Becky gasped. "I just wanted to have a little fun. I didn't think the idiot would get hurt. This is her own fault. She shouldn't have gone out there if she couldn't swim!"

Another lightning bolt struck, closer to the beach.

"There's not a cloud in the sky!" Jimmy yelled as he ran up to find out what was going on. "How is that possible?" he asked nobody in particular, referring to the lightning.

"Who cares?" Nacole said. "We gotta find Grace. She's gone!"

"We're going to need more help than just us if she's lost out there," Jimmy said. "I'm calling 911." He pulled out his cellphone and dialed. "Yes, I'd like to report a missing teen. She fell off a Jet Ski, and we don't know where she went." He spoke for another minute and then hung up. "A rescue team is on the way, guys."

"I feel so helpless," Kent said. "And seriously, look at that fog. It's gotten even thicker."

"It really has," Jimmy agreed. "But look, Kent. It hasn't moved. Doesn't fog, like, move around?"

"Um . . . yeah. That's weird. When I was out there, it was moving so fast I could hardly outrun it." Kent thought for a second. "Now it's just stopped, hiding the whole middle of the lake."

Suddenly, another lightning bolt struck, this one hitting the beach. They all heard the sizzle and felt the thunder deep in their chests.

"I'm getting out of here!" yelled Jimmy.

"Me too!" Becky joined in. She had taken maybe two steps when another bolt of lightning struck her.

"Oh, my God!" Nacole shouted. She ran over to her fallen friend. A few minutes ago she wanted to kill her. Now, she appeared dead.

"She's not breathing! Someone help me!"

Another bolt hit the bar, exploding it into hundreds of fiery pieces. The teens who had been celebrating their graduation were now running for their lives. Most of them went for the parking lot where the cars were, but they didn't get far. More lightning boomed from the sky, bolt after bolt striking down everyone around.

Nacole and Kent took off running. As they got closer to the parking lot, Kent spotted a middle-aged woman slowly walking toward them.

"Stop!" he shouted to her. "Go back to your car and get out of here! It's dangerous!"

"I can't do that," the woman simply said.

"You'll get killed out there!"

"I can't go back," the woman responded. "My daughter is the one doing this."

"What?"

"My daughter, Grace. She's doing this. Get me down to the water. Maybe I can calm her down. Maybe I can stop her."

Kent looked at Nacole in confusion. "Come on," he said after a beat. "Let's go, Nacole!"

Another bolt of lightning crashed from the sky, hitting Elizabeth and Kent together. Nacole ran up to them. Their clothes and skin were burned black. Kent was gone, but Elizabeth was still alive, barely. She reached up toward Nacole, a blackened finger pointing at the girl.

"She . . . is . . . your . . ." Elizabeth gasped. "Grace is your . . ."

Elizabeth's body became lifeless. Bodies were lying everywhere, some smoking and smoldering. Some were alive, some were not. Jimmy somehow hadn't been touched as he looked around in shock. His screams joined the chorus of others, piercing the night. Between the cries, Nacole heard a splash. She looked out to the lake and saw a figure wading up onto the beach, carrying a life jacket.

The figure stepped up onto the sand and dropped the still-tied life preserver with a look of disgust.

"G . . . G . . . Grace?" Nacole stammered out.

Grace ignored Nacole and slowly walked up to her mother's now lifeless corpse.

"Mama, I'm so sorry," Grace whispered, falling to her knees. "You were right. I should have listened. I never should have trusted any of them."

Grace turned her head toward Nacole, her eyes glowing with anger, hate, and power. The look of insanity in Grace's eyes confirmed to Nacole that the Grace who got on the Jet Ski did not come back.

"I trusted you, Nacole," Grace said. "And look what you made me do. You made me kill the only person who ever loved me."

Nacole began to cry. "I didn't know, Grace. Becky had told Kent to take you out in the middle of the lake to mess with you or something," she managed to get out in between hysteric sobs. "I would have stopped them."

"Sure, you would have," Grace shot back, only seeing the terrors her mother warned her about now. "You and your rich-ass friends had this all planned. 'Mess with the retard,' right? Do you think I can't hear? I really liked you . . . but once the motor shut off . . . I knew I'd been tricked. I panicked . . . I couldn't breathe. I guess I passed out and fell in the water. The cold brought me to my senses," she spit out, the hatred taking over. "I don't know how to swim, and of course, the life jacket slipped off me. But I held onto it. I knew I wouldn't let you guys take me out just like that. I knew . . . I knew I'd get my revenge."

Nacole saw the anger swelling up inside of Grace. Her eyes turned fiery as she stood up.

"I slammed my fist into the water and heard a crack of thunder. Water began steaming up into fog all around me. As I held on with all my strength, I could hear Becky laughing coming across the water. I screamed for help, and you all just pointed and laughed."

Grace clenched her fist and raised it over her head as if to strike Nacole. "I hit the water again with my fist, and lightning struck the beach. I realized then that I was somehow doing it. I was controlling the lightning. I heard Becky laugh again, so I pointed my finger at her and made the lightning come down . . . BOOM! She was dead! The lightning was doing what I told it to do. BOOM! BOOM! BOOM! It felt so good! You all would die! BOOM! BOOM! DIE!"

Nacole fell to her knees, shaking violently, feeling as if she were about to throw up.

"Now I know why Mama kept me locked up all those years. She knew. She knew what would happen if I got angry."

Nacole heard sirens coming. "You better go, Grace."

Grace nodded. "It's not safe for me here anymore. I killed all these people. I can't stay here."

Nacole looked at Kent and silently said goodbye. "I want to go with you," she said, reaching out for Grace's hand.

"No," Grace said quietly. "You have to stay here and take care of your little girl."

Nacole stepped back. "What? Grace, I don't have a little girl."

Grace smiled and reached out to Nacole. She gently touched her stomach. "Yes, you do," Grace said. "You're pregnant."

"That's not possible!"

"You know how babies are made. It is possible. You and Kent made a baby."

"How did you know that?"

"I always could tell when people are pregnant. I always thought of it as like a power. Looks like I may have been right about that . . ."

Grace looked thoughtfully at the ground. "I was going to tell you guys on the way home, but um . . . that didn't work out."

Ever curious, Nacole had more questions. "How long have you known? About powers and all that, I mean?"

Grace sighed. "A long time. When I was a little girl, Mama kept me locked up, and I couldn't figure out why. When I was about eight, I got really mad at her and almost killed her. That's when I figured out I was kind of special. Mama told me I couldn't use my powers, but I kept practicing in my bedroom with fire. Almost burned down the house a few times . . . When I turned thirteen, I told Mama I was going to school, and she couldn't stop me. She agreed."

Nacole just shook her head. "So . . . it was your Mama that told you not to talk to anybody? At least that's what you told me."

"It was my idea actually. I promised Mama I wouldn't cause trouble, and not talking to anybody was the only way to make it certain, I thought," Grace admitted. "But when you invited me to the party . . . everything changed. For an instant anyways. I had to come, to see . . . and it turned out exactly as I figured. It was a mess. I knew I'd let you live anyways . . . I wanted you to live for your little girl. I wanted her to know what it felt like to be betrayed . . . to never know her real father . . . but one day, she'll figure it out, Nacole, and she'll be just like me. You'll watch as she gets teased . . . ridiculed . . . forgotten about . . . maybe then you'll know what you and your so-called friends did to me."

"You're crazy, Grace! That makes no sense!"

"Maybe. But I really did care about you. And look what you made me do."

The sirens grew louder. Grace smiled and walked into the lake.

When she was about waist-deep, she turned and looked at Nacole, still smiling. It chilled Nacole right to the bone. Nacole knew at that moment that her friend was as good as gone.

"Grace!" Nacole shouted out. "I have so many questions yet!"

But Grace turned away and walked further into the lake, slipping below the surface and disappearing. Nacole's knees gave out, and she sat down on the sand and started crying.

That's where the first police officer on the scene found her. Other first responders found Jimmy, the only other survivor, but all he could do was howl at them like an animal. Both went to the emergency room, where Nacole tried to tell the story about powers and lightning and fog and betrayal, and a girl named Grace Nelson who had the power to think and destroy. Grace was still missing. Her dead mother was among the victims of the tragedy.

The psychiatrists at the hospital put both of them into a safe, comfortable hospital with acres of well-trimmed lawns. Jimmy and Nacole got lots of therapy, and pretty soon they became best friends. When Nacole had her child, she decided to marry Jimmy, and he adopted the child as his own.

The official inquest into what became known as the "graduation party incident" concluded that a hot Jet Ski exhaust ignited a massive buildup of colorless, odorless, and highly explosive natural gas. Both Jimmy and Nacole testified that Grace had caused all the havoc with her powers, but the panel of inquiry discounted all that as the ravings of traumatized children.

After all, didn't both of those witnesses come from the mental hospital? They had to be crazy after all they went through. Didn't they? Didn't they?

CHAPTER TWO

Thirteen-year-old Mary saw that it was her father calling her mother's phone and picked it up off the counter.

"Hi, Daddy," the vivacious girl said as her mother, Nacole, came into the room. "We've almost got everything packed and ready to move into the new house!"

"That's great, Mary," Jimmy said. "Let me talk to your mom."

The girl handed the phone off to her mother, who still looked the part of the head cheerleader she had been all those years before, before the Graduation Incident at the lake happened.

"Hey, Jimmy," Nacole said. "How close are you to being ready for the furniture?"

"Real close, Nacole," Jimmy replied. "It's gotta be right. Best house I've ever worked on, and it's for us."

Jimmy had become a carpenter, building and remodeling houses, and business was good. Nacole had finished nursing school and now was working at the county hospital. The couple had bought a big, old, rundown farmhouse. Jimmy said it had "good bones." It was close to the hospital, and where it was located, Mary wouldn't go to Wolf County High School. That was important to Jimmy and Nacole. Too many horrible memories.

"Tell you what," Jimmy said. "Let's make Saturday move-in day, OK?"

"Let me put that on speaker. Say that again, Jimmy."

"Let's make Saturday move-in day," Jimmy said again, his voice showing the smile on his face. And Mary let out a squeal.

"Yes! It's really happening!"

Saturday morning, Nacole and Mary made the long drive around the lake in the rented truck full of their furniture and possessions and pulled into the long lane that led to the house. For the first time, Mary really looked at the big old fixer-upper, and she liked what she saw.

It was white, two stories, with a porch that ran the whole width of the house. The porch roof was held up by four giant columns, a look that took her back in time. She got out of the truck and just stood there for a few seconds until she heard her father's voice. She ran around to the back of the house.

"Dad! Dad!" she cried. "You ready for us?" She threw herself into his arms. "We didn't have any TV last night. The TV was in the truck! And Mom made me put everything into boxes." She gave him a pout.

"Oh, poor sweetie," Jimmy said. "Life's so very hard!"

Nacole came around the corner of the house and shook her head. Jimmy hadn't shaved since he started the project.

"You're looking pretty shaggy, sweetheart," she told him.

"Yeah, well, I think I might want to keep this," Jimmy said, stroking the beard. Mary looked horrified.

"Oh, I should tell you, Mary," Jimmy said to her very seriously. "We had to rip out the pool."

"What?" Mary cried out, her eyes wide. "You had to what?"

"I'm just kidding. But . . . we don't have water in it yet. This place has been a lot of work, and we don't have it quite finished."

"But . . . can we move in?" Mary asked, suddenly concerned.

"I'll let you decide. Let's take a look around."

The three walked up the grand porch steps, admiring the freshly painted columns, the recycled-plastic porch floor that would never rot, and the original porch swing, salvaged from the former owners. Jimmy stepped up to the front double door, pushed both sides open, and bowed grandly.

"Ladies, you may enter," he said, showing the way. Nacole and Mary both giggled, stepped inside, and both gasped.

The floor, which had been hidden under an ugly shag carpet, turned out to have gorgeous inlaid hardwood. It shone

41

under a coat of fresh polish. But what drew their attention was a graceful spiral staircase that led to the second floor. Mary hugged herself and began spinning around and around.

"It's like a castle! Our very own castle!" She held out her arms and spun and spun.

"Don't make yourself sick," Jimmy said half seriously. He then picked up the girl and began spinning himself, slowing down gradually. She looked a little dizzy but composed herself well enough to ask where her room was located.

"Well, your dad and I have the master bedroom downstairs," Nacole said. "It's almost as big as our whole old house, and it has its own bath. And we each get our own closet, plus another side room where we can have an office."

"I think you need to see where we'll eat," Jimmy said with some excitement. He led them into a large, formal dining room with the same polished hardwood floor as the front of the house, with French doors that opened up onto the patio.

"We'll need to get the right kind of table, an antique sideboard, and a china cabinet that fits with the house," Nacole said. "Jimmy, is this the kitchen we talked about?"

Jimmy smiled and opened the door. The old kitchen had been completely rebuilt, with stainless-steel appliances, marble countertops, and a professional-style range.

42

"We were able to open up the old windows and get more daylight in here," Jimmy continued. "And it's full LED lighting with just the right amount of warmth to make all the food look so delicious."

"I can't wait to start cooking here," Nacole agreed.

"Daddy!" shouted Mary from the dining room. She had opened up the patio doors to look outside and stood there with a look on her face that was a cross between a little angry and a lot happy. "Daddy, you said you didn't get the swimming pool filled!"

Jimmy laughed out loud and walked out onto the patio, which had as its centerpiece a freshly refurbished pool, the blue water sparkling in the sunshine.

"Just messing with you, pumpkin," he said. "I wondered how long it would take for you to figure it out."

With a broad smile on her face, tears of joy began streaming down. The three of them came together in a full-family multihug by the pool.

"Come on, pretty ladies!" Jimmy finally said. "Let's go see the rest of the house!"

"Daddy," Mary said quickly. "Where's my room? You told me about yours and Mom's. Which one's mine?"

The three walked back through the French doors into the dining room, and Jimmy pointed up. "Oh, it's upstairs. There are four bedrooms up there, actually."

"But which one's mine?" Mary persisted.

"Any one you want," he smiled.

"Are you serious?" Mary squealed in excitement. "You know I'm going to pick the biggest one up there."

"I knew that," Jimmy said as they all ran up the staircase together. "You've got to find it, though."

Mary opened the first door, looked around. It glowed in the light from the open window. She crossed the hall and opened the second door. This room was about the same size as room one, but it had two closets instead of just one. Third door: a lot like the first, but no closets. Just a couple of huge, antique wardrobes.

Then she opened the last door, and she knew she found it.

"Wow," the girl said. A gentle breeze blew through from the windows on two walls; the room was in the corner of the house.

"I love the color scheme," she told her dad. "The light green walls, the dark green curtains; it's great." She pulled the curtains aside and looked out, spotting the neighbor's house down the road, and when she looked down, she saw the patio and pool.

Suddenly, behind her, a toilet flushed. Mary spun around and giggled. "My own bathroom?"

Jimmy opened the door and stepped out. "I thought that was a closet door," Mary added.

"Well," Jimmy said in his best British accent, "the British do call it a 'water closet'." Mary laughed while looking at the fixtures, including her own tub and shower, and a lighted mirror above the vanity. The mirrors were large, and there were lots of drawers in the vanity for whatever Mary wanted to put there.

"I love it!" she said loudly. Jimmy smiled.

"Let's go find your mother."

Nacole was standing in the living room, enjoying the gentle breeze from the ceiling fan and planning where to put the furniture.

"Mom, I love this place," Mary said to her. "My own big room, my own bathroom . . ." A gentle tear started to fall down her face. "Mom, when we get moved in, and when I start school and make some new friends, can I, uh, may I invite some of them over for a pool party?"

"Well, I think your father and I will have to make some plans to invite some of our friends over for a housewarming party." Nacole looked over at Jimmy. "What do you think, Jimmy?"

"I think this will be a great place for our friends," he agreed. "But first, we've got to get moved in."

Mary took that as a yes, and ran back up the spiral staircase to her room. She leaned on the windowsill, looking out across the countryside, and looked at the neighbor's house.

"Is that a man in the upstairs window?" Mary thought. Suddenly, the curtains in that window snapped closed. Mary wasn't sure what she'd seen.

"Wow, that was weird," she thought, as she gently pulled her own curtains back across the window. She walked out the door and began to check out the rest of her castle.

By the next day, the family had almost all of the furniture unloaded, and the stack of boxes in the living room was getting smaller every hour.

"Mom," Mary said, "with a pool and all, I'm going to need a couple of swimsuits. And school's going to start soon. Can we go back-to-school shopping?"

"Oh, I haven't forgotten," Nacole said. "I just didn't want to have to pack up all the new stuff and move it over here. Let's plan to spend Sunday at the mall."

Nacole turned and looked at Mary. "Something I didn't tell you," she said softly. "Your new school requires uniforms."

"What? Like, dumb dresses? I've never worn a dress in my life."

"Well, Mary, consider it part of growing up."

"But my legs are white as flour!" Mary wailed. "I'm going to have to get a tan real fast!"

"You'll be just fine, Punkin," Nacole reassured her. "You have a pool now, so get out there and get you a tan."

"I will. Mom . . . I wish I had some friends to enjoy this with. I miss my old ones."

"I know you do, sweetie. But you'll meet tons of new ones. I promise."

"I hope so." Mary looked lost in her own thoughts. "I sure hope so."

CHAPTER THREE

Late Sunday afternoon, their shopping done, the back seat and cargo area of the SUV filled with shopping bags, the two girls were driving home.

"Mom . . . can I ask you a question?"

"Sure," Nacole replied. "What do you want to know, Punkin?"

"Are you and Dad doing OK?" Mary blurted out. "I mean, you seem to be on the edge a lot lately. And the other night, I heard you downstairs crying. Are you guys all right?"

"Oh, honey," Nacole said finally, smartly changing lanes on the five-lane road. "We're doing fine. Your dad's a rock. It's just me and all the changes we've had, new house, new school, all of that. Plus," Nacole stole a glance at Mary, "you're getting older."

"Why would my getting older make you nervous?" Mary asked. "I don't understand."

Nacole tried to be as casual as she could. "Oh, just something a friend of mine told me a few years ago."

"What's that?" Mary wondered, a concerned look on her face.

"Oh, it's nothing." Mary didn't notice, but a tear or two started running down her mother's face.

"It doesn't sound like nothing," Mary said, reaching into the console, pulling out a tissue, and handing it to her mother. So much for not noticing. Nacole took it, wiped her face, then reached back into the console herself for a cigarette. The light in front of them turned red, and she stopped the SUV. She quickly tapped a Winston out of the package, lit it, and opened the window.

"Mom!" Mary yelled. "I hate it when you smoke. Why'd you ever start?"

"Honey, it just helps me calm my nerves."

"What's wrong with your nerves, Mom? There's got to be something more to it than the new house and new school and me getting older."

Nacole looked straight ahead as the light turned green. She grasped the wheel tightly. Too tightly.

"Mom, your hands are shaking so bad you can barely drive!"

"I'm . . . I'm OK," Nacole stammered. "I mean, I just . . . I just don't want to lose you, Punkin. You're the only kid I got." Nacole tried to smile. "You'll be going to college in a few years, moving away, leaving me all alone, all by myself . . . "

"Dad's here. Is that what you're worried about? I'm not going to leave you. You'll probably have to run me off."

"Well, I hope so," Nacole managed to get out. "Plug in your phone. Let's get some music," signaling the end of that conversation. Mother and daughter listened as they drove to the new house.

It took several trips for Mary to haul all her new clothes upstairs. She dumped the shopping bags on the bed and picked up a new pair of jeans. She skinned off her old jeans, flipped the new ones in the air to pop out any wrinkles, slid them on, and tried hard to fasten them.

She pulled in her stomach and began to get upset. After trying on a few other pairs, she panicked, thinking that the swimsuits would not fit. She put on her old jeans and looked at herself in the mirror.

"I'm . . . faaaaaat!" she cried, the tears starting to flow. She stared into the mirror and screamed.

The mirror shattered.

Mary stood there, stunned, unable to move. She heard footsteps racing up the stairs, and her mother threw open the door. "Are you OK? Why'd you scream? And wow. How'd the mirror get broken?" The mirror had shattered into hundreds of little, pebble-like pieces that lay all over the floor.

"Mom, all my new clothes are too small," Mary cried. "I got fat! I hate myself!"

"Are you serious?" Nacole asked.

"I look so stupid! I've gained all this weight, and I look like a pig!"

"Mary . . . you're growing up. Your body changes every day." Nacole struggled to stay calm. "You are not fat. I don't want to hear you say that about yourself ever again. Look . . . we kept the receipts. We'll just go back tomorrow and exchange these things. It'll all be good." She paused for a moment. "What happened to the mirror?"

"I don't know, Mom," Mary looked confused. "I was really mad and upset and I screamed, and I must have knocked into it somehow . . ."

Nacole looked at what was left of the mirror. It was six feet tall with a solid hardwood frame and plywood back. The glass was shattered completely out of the frame. It looked as if it had crumbled like a cookie.

"I didn't mean to break it!" Mary said loudly and began to cry all over again.

"Calm down, Mary, calm down. It must have been defective. Your dad knows the guys at the glass company. We'll be able to replace it."

"So you're not mad? I didn't mean to break it."

"Accidents happen, Mary. We'll get a new one. Now just get dressed, and come down and help me with supper. I want to show off my marble countertops!"

Nacole left the room, and Mary, stepping carefully around the shards of glass, finished getting dressed and then followed her mother downstairs to help her make dinner in their new kitchen.

After supper, Mary brought a broom and dustpan upstairs, planning to sweep up the glass. But she set it aside, deciding instead to put the clothes she planned to return back into the right stores' shopping bags. But she kept returning to the mirror, the glittery mess on the floor of her new bedroom.

"I didn't touch that mirror," she thought. "I wasn't even that close to it." She began searching her mind for an answer, staring at the glass. One piece caught her attention for some reason, and she stared hard at it, really hard. Her face hardened. Her eyes darkened.

The broken glass moved.

"Did that just happen?" Mary thought, in shock. "Am I seeing things?" She crouched down and picked up the piece of mirror. She looked at her reflection in the shard, and dropped it suddenly. Mary stared again at the pile of glass on the floor, stared hard, and the whole pile of pieces began to writhe and dance. Mary gasped, her mouth gone dry.

"How's this possible?" she asked herself. The broken glass was still dancing on the floor, and a few pieces were starting to float up as if they were in zero gravity in space. More shards took off, and soon there was a train of silvery, sharp glass circling Mary, once, twice, three times, then gently descending toward the pile on the floor.

"This is crazy!" Mary said out loud. She covered her eyes, broke her concentration, and all the glass clattered to the floor. "What the hell is going on?"

Mary stumbled over to her new desk, pulled out the chair, and sat down. She put her elbows on her knees, her chin in her hands, and found herself breathing heavily.

"This is really crazy," Mary said again. "I thought stuff like this only happened in fairy tales." She had an idea. "If this is a fairy tale . . ." she thought.

Mary got up and stood in front of the empty mirror frame. She focused on the pile of glass on the floor, and once again, the pieces started to writhe and dance. Then Mary imagined the mirror as it was, all the pieces in place where they once were. The shards again took off and began to circle in space, round and round her, but instead of landing back on the floor, the pieces landed back in the mirror frame. Like a giant, glittery, silvery jigsaw puzzle, the chunks of glass put themselves back together again, welding themselves together so well no one could tell they had ever been apart.

Mary sat down hard in the chair. The mirror quivered a little, then stayed quiet.

Mary began to jump up and down, letting out little squeals of delight. "I did it!" she thought. "I really did it!" But then she thought, "How am I going to explain this to Mom?" Still, she couldn't help but want to play with her new power.

She sat down again and stared at the bookcase. A couple of books began to quiver, then lifted a little bit and slid out.

"Focus, Mary, focus."

Suddenly, one of the books fell to the floor, but the other moved steadily through the air across the room.

"This way. This way," Mary thought. She put up her hand, and the book almost seemed to sense where it was going. She smiled, and the book picked up speed and smacked into her hand, almost hard enough to hurt.

"I did it!" she said out loud. "I think I got this figured out."

Mary stayed up the rest of the night focusing on every piece of furniture in her room.

CHAPTER FOUR

The next day, after Mary and Nacole made another trip to the mall to return the clothes that didn't fit, Nacole was in the kitchen. She heard a knock on the door, answered it, and saw a dark-haired girl about Mary's age standing there.

"Well, hi," Nacole said. "Who are you?"

"My name's Rachel," the girl said. "I live across the road in the red brick house, and I saw you guys moving in. I saw a girl packing in boxes. Is that your daughter?"

"Sure is," Nacole smiled. "Her name's Mary." Rachel looked around.

"Your house is so beautiful," Rachel said.

"Thank you," Nacole said. "My husband's been working on it for a while, and I'm glad he got it in move-in condition before school starts." She paused. "Would you like to come in? You would probably like to meet Mary."

"Thank you. I do!" Rachel said, her eyes widening as she spotted the spiral staircase leading upstairs.

"Mary!" Nacole called out. "Come downstairs for a minute!"

"What do you need, Mom?" came Mary's voice from upstairs.

"It's the girl from across the street," Nacole shouted back. "She wants to meet you!"

"Don't let her get away!" Mary called back, quickly appearing at the top of the stairs and spinning down as fast as she could. "I'm Mary," she said, a little out of breath, pulling her blond hair into a ponytail then holding out her hand.

Rachel took Mary's hand and shook it firmly. "I'm Rachel," she said. "Welcome to . . ." She kind of looked all around. "I guess this place doesn't have a name. It's just home. So welcome home!"

The two girls giggled. "So where did you all move from?" Rachel asked.

"We used to live on the other side of the lake, but my mom and dad didn't want me to go to Wolf County High, so we moved here."

"Why don't they want you to go to Wolf County High?"

"Mom and Dad don't really talk about it, but I guess something really bad happened before I was born, and I've heard about a gas explosion that killed a bunch of kids on graduation night. But Mom and Dad were okay. Let's go upstairs to my room!"

Nacole quietly smiled and nodded as the two girls took off for the spiral stairs. *Maybe someday,* she thought, heading back to the kitchen.

Mary and Rachel went into Mary's room, and the dark-haired girl just looked around in awe. "It's so big!" Rachel said.

Mary smiled. "And I've got my own bathroom."

"You're spoiled," Rachel smiled.

"I'm Daddy's girl," Mary said. "He said I could have whatever room I wanted, so I picked this one. Besides, Mom and Dad are downstairs, and who else is going to pick it?"

"I'm jealous. Can I come and live with you?" Rachel teased.

"Do you like to swim?" Mary asked. Rachel nodded.

"I sure do," Rachel said. Mary pulled open the curtains.

"Then you're going to love the pool!" Mary said. Rachel shrieked with glee.

"Dad told me when I make some friends, I can invite them over to swim any time I want," Mary said. "And you're invited."

Rachel hugged Mary, and the two girls danced around the room. Turning serious, Mary asked, "So when does school start?"

"In a few days," Rachel responded. "My mom knows the exact day."

"So what's it like? Any cute boys?" Mary asked.

"Oh yes," Rachel said. "Tons of them. There's this one boy, named Tommy. He's got dark eyes, beautiful skin, and the most beautiful smile. And there's Daniel. He's real muscular, brown hair, and a great smile, too. He's gorgeous."

"Do you know them?" Mary asked.

"Sure I do," Rachel said. "They're like my best friends."

"Will you introduce me to them?"

"Sure," Rachel said. "So what about the not-so-good-looking guys for the not-so-good-looking girls like me?" Mary asked.

Mary sat on the bed and gave a little pout. Rachel put her arms around her. "You're not ugly. Not at all. I think you will do okay with the boys."

"Just okay?" Mary's pout got a little bigger.

"Okay, you'll do great," Rachel said, pulling her new friend close, then tossing her onto the bed. Mary jumped down beside her, and the two girls began tickling each other. Both began giggling as they wrestled all over Mary's bed.

"Okay, Rachel, you win!" Mary declared.

Mary arched her back and lowered her head with a devious grin, then she proceeded to tackle Rachel once again and pinned her down onto the mattress.

This caused Rachel to scream, "Stop it, Mary, you're hurting me!" Despite the screaming, she had a slight giggle in her voice.

"Quit lying, you devious little girl," Mary said just a little bit louder than a whisper.

"I give! You win!" Rachel wailed.

Mary rolled off the top of Rachel, and both girls lay quietly with their backs flat on Mary's mattress.

"I can't breathe," Rachel declared, trying laboriously to catch her breath.

"Me either!" Mary replied.

"But that was really fun!" Rachel said. Both of the girls stood quietly and stared at the floor. Both of them were simply at a loss for words.

"So what grade are you going into?" Rachel asked.

"Mm-hmm, ninth grade, and I'm really excited for high school to start."

"I am too! How old are you?" Rachel asked.

"Thirteen, but I'll be fourteen in December."

Rachel then needled her new acquaintance and remarked, "So that means that I'll be getting my driver's license before you!"

Mary, sensing a bit of a challenge, couldn't help but respond back in a way that almost found common ground between the two girls.

"No way! I guess that means we're just going to have to find a couple of cute boys with cars to drive us around, now won't we?"

"And these boys you told me about, how old are they?" Mary asked.

"They're both sophomores. I don't know their actual ages," Rachel replied with a coy grin on her face and a hint of deviousness in her voice.

Mary sensed Rachel's infatuation and shifted the subject. "So what are you doing tomorrow?" Rachel asked.

"My mom and I are going into town to pick up the last of my school stuff. I hope it doesn't take too long because you know how moms can be sometimes."

Mary chuckled and replied, "Oh, I definitely know about that. While you're there, you better go shopping for a couple of new swimsuits. You're going to need them for the pool."

Rachel responded with genuine relief in her voice. "Oh my gosh, I would have totally forgotten! I'm so happy you reminded me. What kind of suit do you wear? One piece or two?"

Mary responded without hesitation, "Definitely two. I don't care what anybody thinks about me."

Rachel, aware of the time, replied, "I'm definitely with you on that! Look, I better be going so I can get home before my mom sends out a search party looking for me."

As Rachel turned to head for the door, she stopped mid-stride, turned around, and looked at Mary. "Good night, Mary. I'll see you tomorrow, just as soon as I can get here."

CHAPTER FIVE

Rachel woke up the next morning to the smell of her mother's freshly brewed coffee downstairs. She pulled on her jeans and a T-shirt and ran downstairs.

"Hi, Mom! Can I have a cup of coffee?" she chirped.

Elizabeth, her mother, looked over the top of her glasses at her daughter. "You may have a cup of coffee as soon as you're old enough to get a real job," the older woman said.

"OK, Mom . . . ," Rachel said. It wasn't the first time she and her mother had this conversation, and it wouldn't be the last. "I know we're going shopping today, Mom, and don't forget we need to get me a couple of swimsuits so I can go over to Mary's house and swim in her pool. And since I'm already ready to go, may I please go over to Mary's house for just a little bit? When you're ready, I'll come right back if that's OK with you, Mom."

Elizabeth just smiled. It was good to see her daughter excited about her new friend, especially with school about to start and Rachel getting ready to start her freshman year at high school. Elizabeth knew this wouldn't be grade school any more.

"Sure, kiddo," Elizabeth said. "Tell you what; I'll just pull into the neighbor's driveway and honk the horn when I'm ready. Go head over there now," Elizabeth said. "Love you, kiddo."

"Love you too, Mom!" Rachel said, racing for the door.

Rachel dashed across the road and knocked on the door of Mary's house. Nacole smiled broadly when she saw who it was.

"Hey, Rachel, go on upstairs and knock on the door—you know the way."

The girl sped up the spiral stairs and knocked on Mary's door. Inside, she heard a radio playing softly, and it was playing her favorite song! She knocked again, and Mary told her to come in. Mary was in her bathrobe, fresh out of the shower.

"I can't believe you're here," Mary said. "Come sit next to me on the bed." Rachel sat down, and Mary put her arms around Rachel.

"Listen to the radio," Mary said. "That's my favorite song."

Rachel gasped, "Mine too!" She put her head on Mary's shoulder, and the two of them listened to the song until it ended, and the morning zoo team of disc jockeys began laughing annoyingly at their own jokes. Mary turned down the radio, and Rachel whispered into Mary's ear.

"That song has to be our song forever. That has to be some kind of sign that we're supposed to be best friends forever."

"Maybe," Mary said. Rachel's face fell.

"What do you mean, maybe?" Rachel said. Mary stood up and pulled the bathrobe a little tighter around herself.

"I don't know, I mean, I hope so but," Mary stammered, "I mean, I . . ."

"B-b-but what?" Rachel said, her eyes getting misty. Mary looked away.

"What am I supposed to say?" Mary said. "I mean, I hope so, but I can't bring myself to believe in destiny."

"Why not?"

"Well, just because we like the same songs and maybe the same food doesn't mean we're going to be best friends forever."

Rachel pouted a little. "Well, you could have gone with it for me," she said. "I thought that moment was perfect." Rachel looked closely at her friend, who was just staring out into space. "What's wrong, Mary?"

Mary shook her head a little and pulled the robe a little tighter around herself as if she were cold.

"I don't know; I've been having these really bad dreams for about a week now," Mary said. "I don't know what they mean."

"Like how bad?"

"Bad," Mary said. "Burned bodies, people screaming and running everywhere on fire—it's all about to drive me crazy."

Rachel gasped. She stood up to hug her friend, but Mary moved away just a little.

"And the worst part is this woman is telling me that she's my Aunt Grace," Mary said. "I don't have an Aunt Grace. And my mom's in the dreams too, kneeling at the top of the burned bodies . . ." Mary broke down into tears. This time, when Rachel hugged her, she didn't move away.

"I haven't told Mom or anyone else," Mary said.

Rachel wiped the tears from Mary's face with her fingertips, and with compassion in her voice, said, "I'm so sorry, Mary."

Mary shuddered a little and responded. "That Aunt Grace woman scares me. She told me that the man my mother was kneeling next to was my dad." Mary continued, "Rachel, my dad's not dead! He's here, right downstairs. Does that mean he's going to die?" Mary's tears started flowing once again. Rachel did her best to comfort Mary and said:

"Nobody's going to hurt you either. It was only a dream; I promise that I won't let anyone hurt you."

"Promise?" Mary asked, looking for reassurance.

Rachel said, "I promise. Now go get dressed."

Mary smiled, turned, and started to walk to the bathroom to change her clothes.

"So, what are you going to do today while I'm gone?" Rachel asked, continuing the conversation in an attempt to distract and comfort Mary.

"I think I might go out on the patio and lay out so I can catch a little sun on this uber-white skin of mine."

"Shut up!" Rachel responded, stomping her feet and puckering her lip. "Now I want to stay here with you, Mary, and lay out with you!"

Mary snickered audibly from inside the bathroom and teased her friend. "Oh, quit acting like a little crybaby; what would you lay out in anyway—your undies?"

Rachel grinned and pictured the scene that Mary had just described, and replied with a subtle grin on her face, "I guess you're right. I guess I'll just worry about you all day then."

Mary smiled, touched by her friend's concern. "Rachel . . . I'll be fine. Besides, I'm feeling better after talking to you and telling you about my dreams. I hope they don't come back."

Rachel couldn't help but agree with her friend and said, "I hope so too."

As Mary continued to change in the bathroom, Rachel turned and walked toward the window and opened the long green curtains. As she did, a stream of morning sunshine flooded into the room.

Mary had finished changing by this point and had walked over to the window where Rachel was standing. As both girls looked out the window, Mary found herself looking at the white house that had caught her attention last time. Without taking her gaze off the white house that stood next door, she asked Rachel.

"Who lives in that white house over there?"

"That's just John," Rachel replied. "He's real good friends with our family. Mom and Dad think the world of him."

"He's been friends with our family ever since I was born," Rachel said. "I used to go over to his house and play almost every day." Mary couldn't quite tell why, but she didn't like that answer.

"So why did you stop?" Mary asked.

"Well, you showed up."

"Is he married?"

"No, he lives by himself."

"Wow!" Mary found that really weird. "And your mom lets you go over to his house and play by yourself?" she asked.

"Sure, why not?" Rachel responded. "They trust him. He's a sweet guy."

"I bet he is," Mary thought. "Look how close his house is to ours," Mary said. "I bet he could look into my room from that upstairs window from across the way. I'm not going to be able to keep my curtains open. This is creepy!"

"Mary," Rachel said, with a pleading tone in her voice, "do me a favor, please. Don't talk to him or hang around him." Mary wasn't sure why, but this was setting off alarm bells in her head.

"Why? Why would you say that?" Mary demanded.

"Well, I haven't talked to him since you folks moved in," Rachel said. "And I'm afraid he'll be mad. He has a temper . . ."

"Mary, you don't understand," Rachel said. "I'm the only friend he's ever had, and I've been going over to his house pretty much every day for years. I don't know how he's going to react if I start hanging around with you all the time."

"If you're trying to scare me, Rachel, it's not going to work!" Mary said.

"I know," Rachel shot back. "But just stay away from him, for me." A tear formed at the edge of Rachel's eye.

"Okay, Rachel," Mary sighed. "For you, but John better not start anything—with me or with you—or that'll be the last time he tries." Rachel knew Mary wasn't bluffing, just as Mary knew there was more going on with John and Rachel than she was letting on.

"Is there something I need to know?" Mary asked.

"No," Rachel replied a little too quickly. "Why?"

"You just started acting a little strange when I brought him up."

"There's nothing, I promise."

"If there were something, you'd tell me, right?" Mary said.

"Sure." Rachel's eyes wouldn't meet Mary's. Suddenly, she noticed the full-length mirror that had been in Mary's room wasn't there anymore.

"What happened to your mirror?"

"It broke—or actually, it cracked," Mary said. "Dad took it back to the glass company to get the mirror replaced."

"Wow! How'd it crack?"

Mary, with a bewildered look on her face, said, "I don't know. I was just trying on my new clothes, and it just cracked all over. Maybe it thought I was fat and ugly."

"Well, that's just bad luck. But I don't think you're fat or ugly."

Rachel changed the subject and said, "So school starts tomorrow."

"Yeah, I am really kind of nervous," Mary responded, shrugging her shoulders.

"It's going to be different," Rachel continued, trying to comfort Mary. "You'll be okay, I promise you that. I'll always be there to protect you."

Mary looked at Rachel and asked, "Do I look like I need protecting?"

"Oh, you need protecting from the evil demons and zombies that lurk around our school and come after girls like you," Rachel said.

Mary, looking simply disgusted, replied, "You know what I need? I need someone to keep me from running into the mean kids and teachers and to make sure I'm introduced to all the cute boys! But seriously, your school makes us wear uniforms, right? I'm worried I'm going to look so stupid in a skirt! I don't even know how to wear a skirt! I'm going to end up showing everything to the entire world!"

"Just don't bend over to tie your shoes, and when you sit down, make sure you cross your legs like a lady. If you do all that, you'll be just fine," Rachel giggled.

The girls' conversation was soon interrupted by a car horn.

"That's my mom; I have to go."

Rachel stood up and brushed herself off, straightening her clothes. "It sure would be nice to have a mirror," she grumbled.

Mary just rolled her eyes. "When will you be back?" Mary asked.

"I don't know," Rachel said. "Whenever my mom gets done shopping. It's hard to tear her away from stores."

"Come over when you get done," Mary pleaded.

"I will."

The two girls hugged each other goodbye, almost as if they were leaving each other for weeks. Rachel spiraled down the stairs, out the front door, and into the car. Mary watched them drive off, closed the curtains, and then walked to her bed. This was going to be a lonely day, and school starts tomorrow. The day wore on as she continued to lounge around in her room. Mid-afternoon, her phone buzzed. Her face lit up when she saw it was a text from Rachel.

"BOOOORING!" Rachel texted.

"U still shoping?" Mary wrote.

"Mom has to see everything in every shop in the whole mall."

"When will you guys be done?"

"Dunno."

"Well, call me as soon as you get done shopping."

"Mom just found something she wants to show me got to go bye."

CHAPTER SIX

The alarm went off—way too early. Mary pushed the snooze button, dozed for another five minutes, then pushed the button again. The clock wouldn't give up, however, so finally, she did and got out of bed. She yawned, sat up, and then thought of Rachel. She was still thinking about their long, late-night phone conversation from last night.

The alarm went off again. This time, Mary turned it off and stood up. The floor was cold on her bare feet, and she stumbled into the bathroom. Mary looked into the mirror, saw the bags under her eyes, and knew she'd been up way too late.

She was starting to feel a little sick. This was not good. Mary stepped into the shower, and the hot water felt good. But not good enough. Her mind was racing. First day of school. All the new kids. That horrible school uniform. Ugh!

"Mom!" she called out, louder than she intended. "Are you making breakfast?"

Mom's voice drifted upstairs. "I'm just getting started. Do you want something special for today?"

"Oh, no," Mary called back. "Just cereal." Mary grabbed her hair dryer and began to blow-dry her hair. It wasn't cooperating. Mary was still fighting with her hair when Nacole appeared at the door. She gently took the brush from the girl's hand, and somehow, the way only moms knew how, Mary's hair began to behave. Mary got up, pulled on her new white blouse, then stepped into her brand-new school uniform skirt. Nacole covered her smile as her daughter struggled to make the uniform fit just right.

"Mom, I look stupid!" Mary wailed, rolling her eyes.

"You look fine," Nacole said. "You're going to be the prettiest girl in high school."

"That's a lie, Mom. Rachel's prettier than me. And I look stupid. And I'm going to hate school. And I won't make any new friends. Mom!"

Nacole took her daughter's hands in hers and looked into the girl's eyes, which were already full of tears.

"You'll be OK," Nacole reassured her. "And Rachel went to school with a lot of these kids, and she'll be right there with you."

"Thank God for Rachel," Mary finally said. "I'd die without her."

Mary blinked back the tears, straightened her shoulders, and held even tighter to her mother's hands. Nacole picked up the hairbrush and ran it through Mary's hair. She turned her daughter around.

"It's time. Go to school after you get something to eat."

"Yes, Mom," Mary agreed, knowing she wouldn't win this one. Mary hugged her mom one more time and ran out the door and down the stairs.

By the time Nacole followed her down the spiral stairs, Mary had already run to the kitchen, filled a bowl with cereal, and gobbled it down. As Nacole arrived, Mary was wiping her mouth. She picked up her bag and headed to the door.

"Stop," Nacole said, reaching for her phone. "Look at me." She took a quick photo. "Now come here." The two hugged, and Nacole took a couple selfies with her. Mary ran to the door.

"You look beautiful," Nacole told her daughter. "Is Rachel meeting you at the bus stop?" "Yes, I can hardly wait!" Mary ran across the road as the school bus appeared just as Rachel came out of her house. Rachel motioned for Mary to head a few hundred feet down the road to an area designated as the bus stop for the little settlement. The two climbed aboard, and Rachel motioned to Mary to go all the way to the back of the bus.

"This way we can see who else gets on the bus," Rachel explained. "And by the way, I think you look great for your first day."

"Shut up! I still have to get a tan. You're the beautiful one." Rachel stuck out her tongue in response.

"Seriously," Mary said. "Now I'm scared."

"No reason to be scared," Rachel assured her. "You're going to be OK."

"How do you know that?"

"Because you have me," Rachel explained. "I called the school yesterday and talked to the principal, who's really nice. I told him you just moved here, didn't know anybody, and you were worried. He arranged to put you in all of my classes. We'll never be apart!"

"Why didn't I think of that?"

"Because you're not as smart as me," Rachel teased.

Mary watched as more students piled onto the bus. Rachel waved at some of them.

"Do you know all these kids?" Mary asked.

"No," Rachel answered, "but we will."

When the bus arrived at school, it pulled into the big, circular driveway in front of the school. Rachel got out and hopped onto the sidewalk. She then threw her head back and howled like a wolf. Mary looked confused. Rachel howled again.

"Wh ... what? Why?" Mary asked.

"I'm howling!" Rachel stated the obvious. "C'mon girl! Loosen up! And look! Right over there! That's Tommy and Daniel!"

"Where?"

"Those two guys over there by the tree," Rachel said, pointing to where two seemingly handsome guys stood.

"The cute ones," said Rachel, again stating the obvious.

"What are you doing?" Mary asked urgently. "They'll see us!"

"That's the goal! Here they come!" The two boys walked up to Rachel and Mary.

"Hey guys! What's up?" Rachel asked.

"Not much," one of the boys said. "You girls excited for the first day of school?"

"It's a school," Rachel said, rolling her eyes. "Guys, this is Mary. She's new here. Be nice to her. Mary, this is Tommy and this is Daniel." Tommy nodded, and Daniel stared, making serious eye contact and half-smiling.

"No problem," Daniel said. "None at all."

Rachel dug an elbow into Mary's side. "Invite them," she hissed.

That broke the spell for a second. "Um, yeah, OK," Mary mumbled back. "Uh ... listen ... guys ..."

"Mary really can talk," Rachel cut in, easing her friend's discomfort. "What she's trying to say is that she and her family just moved in, they have a pool, and you're invited to her first pool party."

"What she said," Mary agreed. "You guys are invited. It's in a few days."

"Oh, yeah, that sounds like fun," Tommy said. "I'm going to have to ask my parents first before I can say for sure."

"Me too," Daniel said, still staring at Mary.

"Yeah, sure. Let me know. We'll have plenty of food, and the pool's really cool," Mary stammered out.

"Sounds good!" Tommy said. "Daniel ... Daniel!"

"Uh, yeah, food," he smiled. "I'll ask Mom."

"We'll see you girls later," Tommy said.

"Please come," Mary pleaded. "It really will be fun."

As the boys left, Mary turned to Rachel. "They are gorgeous!"

"Why didn't you just grab his hand to hold him hostage?" Rachel teased. "I got a lot of work to do on your flirting skills, Mary."

"We didn't have guys like that at my old school."

"I told you they were hot."

The rest of the day went by in a blur for both of the girls. Changing classes, meeting a half-dozen new teachers, occasionally running into Daniel and Tommy, and figuring out how the cafeteria worked was all brand new. Finally, the two found themselves back on the bus, heading home.

"This was way different than elementary school," Mary said. "And really different from public schools, too."

"Well, the Academy's pretty special," Rachel responded.

"I'll never get used to wearing a dress," Mary complained.

"It's not even a dress, silly. It's a skirt and blouse."

"Whatever." Mary rolled her eyes.

CHAPTER SEVEN

Rachel tossed her backpack over her shoulder, crossed the street, and knocked on Mary's door. Nacole came to the door and smiled when she saw who it was.

"Hello, Rachel," Nacole said. "Come on in."

"I came over a little early to help Mary get ready for today's party," Rachel said. "How can I help?"

"Actually, we've got most everything ready," Nacole said. "You guys are going to have so much fun!"

Rachel was about to go upstairs when Nacole added, "Have you ever met my husband, Jimmy?"

"No, ma'am," Rachel said. "But I'd like to." Nacole walked back to the kitchen and returned with Jimmy.

"Jimmy, this is Rachel, the girl across the street that Mary keeps talking about," Nacole said. Rachel put out her hand, and Jimmy shook it. He was pleased and a little surprised by the girl's firm handshake.

"Good to meet you, sir," Rachel said. "I really like your daughter. She's become my best friend in the whole world!"

Jimmy laughed. "Well, I think you've become Mary's best friend in the whole world," he said. "You're all she talks about. And you don't have to call me sir. Call me Jimmy."

"OK, sir—I mean, Jimmy."

"I'm really glad you two hit it off," Jimmy said. "She really needed a friend, moving to a new place and starting a new school. It's really tough doing it all by yourself."

"I've never tried to do anything like that, Jimmy. I've lived here all my life," Rachel said.

"We're so glad you came over and introduced yourself. Why don't you go upstairs and see how Mary's doing?" Nacole added.

Rachel responded, "I think I'll do that."

As Rachel turned, she said, "It was really nice to meet you, Jimmy." Rachel continued toward the spiral staircase, and when she reached the top, she discovered that Mary's door was locked. Rachel knocked.

Mary heard the knock on her door and called out, "I'm in the bathroom! Come on in!" Rachel turned the knob and found it wouldn't turn.

"Mary, I think the door is locked."

In a few moments, the door clicked open, and there stood Mary in front of the door in a white two-piece swimsuit.

"WOW ... I love how the white swimsuit sets off your incredible tan," Rachel giggled.

Mary punched Rachel in the shoulder and exclaimed, "SHUT UP! You know I haven't had a chance to get some sun. I'm white as a ghost!"

Rachel then opened up her backpack and pulled out her swimsuit. It was a white two-piece.

"You got a white one too?" Mary gasped.

Rachel smiled and ran into Mary's bathroom, closed the door, and emerged quickly wearing her new suit that was a little like Mary's.

"Last time I was here, I saw your swimsuit laying out on your bed, and I really liked it. So I decided to get one like yours. Do you like it?"

"Yes, and I so wish I had your body!"

"Really?" Rachel asked, then made a counterpoint to her friend's insecurities. "At least you've got boobs and a butt." Both girls started to giggle.

Mary interrupted the giggling with a reminder of the time. "Well, we better get downstairs."

Both girls took deep breaths, composed themselves, and headed downstairs to the kitchen.

As the girls reached the kitchen, Mary's mom was there. Mary innocently asked, "Mom, do you need help with anything?"

Nacole turned and looked at the girls. "It's all good. Why don't you girls go out to the patio and see if your dad needs help with anything?"

Out on the patio, Jimmy had fired up the grill and was cooking hot dogs and burgers with a big pot of baked beans on the side burner.

"Oh, hey, girls," Jimmy said as they came out onto the patio area where he was cooking. "Why don't you grab the cups, paper plates, and silverware and set up the buffet on the picnic table?"

Nacole had set all of the supplies they needed near the patio door, and the two girls picked up a roll of plastic to cover the table, along with a half-dozen flexible plastic clamps to keep the plastic from blowing off the table. The girls worked together to cover the table in preparation for the barbecue feast that Jimmy was preparing for them.

The girls quickly set up the buffet table. All that remained was to bring the burgers and hot dogs from the grill, where Jimmy was keeping them warm.

"Hey, Dad," Mary said. "Are any of your or Mom's friends coming to the party today?"

"No, Mary, it'll be just your new friends from the Academy," Jimmy said. He smiled at the two girls, and Rachel smiled right back with her best smile. Mary looked at her friend and suddenly realized that Rachel was giving her dad the eye.

"Rachel..." Mary started to say.

"Your dad is hot," Rachel whispered. "Great bod, blond hair, blue eyes... wow, he's every young girl's dream!"

Mary was shocked. This was her dad Rachel was talking about!

"I don't think he'd like you," Mary said.

"And why not?"

"He likes long-haired blondes with a nice chest," Mary said. "You're a brunette with short hair, and you're flat."

"For now."

Mary just shook her head. She couldn't believe her best friend was suddenly hot for her dad. Her dad!

"Can I ask him?" Rachel said hopefully.

"No!" Mary said. "What's wrong with you? Are you crazy? What would my mom say if she saw you flirting with him?"

"Ok, ok, I promise I'll quit," Rachel groaned.

"So, how many people do you think will show up today?"

"Well, I handed out like about twenty paper invitations, and I put it up online," Mary said. "But I don't know how many

Academy kids have friended me yet. If they've friended me, they'll see it."

"Well, some kids should get the idea and show up," Rachel said. "We'll just have to wait and see."

"Want to go swimming while we're waiting?" Mary asked.

"Sure!" Both girls made a beeline for the pool and jumped in. Pretty soon, they were splashing each other and giggling wildly.

"The water's perfect!" Rachel called out. "I love it!" She spotted Mary's dad up on the patio. "Hey, Jimmy, why don't you join us?"

Jimmy shook his head. "I've got to be ready to let people in," he said, then winked at Rachel. She gave him a little-girl pout.

"OK," she said.

"Maybe later," Jimmy smiled. Mary gave her friend an evil look.

"Would you quit flirting with my dad?" Mary whispered. She smacked Rachel lightly on the back of the head, then pushed her under for a second. Rachel came up sputtering.

"I can't help it," she finally said. "Your dad is so good-looking. I wonder what it would be like to kiss an older man."

"Stop that!" Mary said. "Better not let Mom catch you flirting with her husband! If she catches you, I'm getting out of Dodge!"

Rachel looked hurt. "You wouldn't stay here and defend me? I'd stay with you."

"Sure you would," Mary said.

The girls then heard Jimmy call out, "I think some people are here. I'm going to answer the door."

Mary froze. "Now what do I do?"

"Just calm down, be cool, and please don't be desperate," Rachel said, assuming the role of the big sister.

"I can't help it," Mary said. "I'm excited, scared. What if it's Daniel and Tommy? I'll die right there..."

Jimmy came out of the patio door, followed by a group of young people. He pointed to the pool and the picnic table. Mary's eyes widened.

"I, uh, don't know any of these kids' names!" she said.

"No problem!" Rachel said, quickly climbing out of the pool and grabbing a towel. "Hey, guys, we need to help Mary with names!"

Mary climbed out, looking a little dazed. Rachel continued, "This is Brenda," Rachel said, pointing. "And Kristin, and Summer. And the boy is Erick. The man who let you in is Mary's dad, Jimmy, and the woman over by the table is her mom, Nacole."

"Glad you could come!" Nacole said. "We've got burgers and hot dogs, but why don't you guys jump in the pool? It's nice and warm!"

Everyone was wearing swimwear underneath their street clothes, so they just peeled off what they didn't need, dropped it on the chairs by the pool, and dove in. A few minutes later, Jimmy delivered another group of kids to the pool, and Rachel made more introductions. She was starting to like doing that.

Mary was starting to get comfortable and remember more names. She'd met these kids in class, and she was starting to put things together. Then Daniel and Tommy showed up.

"Hey, Mary! Hey, Rachel!" Daniel called out. "Hey, everybody! We made it!"

"Cool!" Rachel said. Mary's mouth opened, but no words came out. Rachel elbowed her in the ribs. "Say hi!" Rachel whispered.

"Hi, guys!" Mary said weakly. "Uh, jump in. The water's nice and warm." They didn't need any more encouragement, and pretty soon the pool was full of splashing young teenagers.

Rachel kept sneaking looks at Jimmy, who now was wearing only cutoffs and flip-flops, and Mary kept giving her friend evil looks. No one seemed to notice.

After an hour or so, some of the teens began to climb out of the pool and dry themselves off. Mary climbed out, all smiles, with Rachel right behind her. And that's when Rachel saw the red spot on Mary's swimsuit bottom.

"Mary," Rachel whispered. "You've started your period."

"Oh, no," Mary said. "Now what do I do?" She started to cry.

"I've got you," Rachel said. "Just walk on the other side of me. We'll get our towels and get upstairs. Now move, girl!"

The two of them had almost gotten to the chair with the towels on it when one of the boys started laughing. Rachel saw it was Erick and gave him a dirty look. It didn't matter. He stood up and pointed. "Hey, everybody, look! Mary's started her period."

He pointed to Mary's bottom. "Bloody Mary! Bloody Mary!"

Several of the other kids joined in. "Bloody Mary! Bloody Mary!"

Mary felt the rage well up inside her. She looked down at the paving stones on the patio, then up at Erick. When they saw the look on Mary's face, the young teens stopped mid-chant. Rachel put her hand on Mary's shoulder.

"Don't touch me!" Mary said, roughly shoving her friend's hand away. Mary clenched her fists, her hands shaking, her eyes growing dark and fierce.

"C'mon, Mary, we gotta get in the house," Rachel pleaded.

The wind started blowing, stronger and stronger, strong enough to flip over the table with its plates and cups. The wind blew even stronger, and Rachel saw that the water in the pool had somehow turned blood-red. The kids started screaming.

"Get in the house, now!" Jimmy cried. They didn't need any encouragement.

"Mary!" Rachel called over the gale-force wind. "Mary! You gotta move!" But Mary stood still as a statue, staring at where Erick had been, debris flying all over the yard. Rachel finally grabbed Mary and began pushing her toward the house.

"Come on! We gotta get you inside!" Rachel said. She grabbed someone's towel as it flew by, wrapped it around Mary's waist, and pushed her toward the door. Somehow, they got inside and up the spiral staircase. Neither girl saw where the other kids had gone. Rachel got Mary into her room.

"I hate them," Mary growled. "I hate them all. They'll get what's coming to them. I hate them. I hate them. I hate them."

"Mary, what happened out there?" Rachel asked.

"They made me angry," Mary said in the quietest, coldest voice Rachel had ever heard. "They shouldn't make me angry."

Rachel shuddered and tried not to think about anything she'd heard or seen. She took a deep breath.

"We've got to get you cleaned up," Rachel finally said. "We've got to get you into the shower."

"You scared me to death," Rachel said.

"Well, I guess I kind of went into shock or something when the kids started laughing at me, and I don't remember anything that happened after that," Mary said. "How did I get upstairs?"

"I got you here," Rachel said. "Now, you have to get cleaned up."

"Where are the kids now?" Mary said.

"I don't know," Rachel said. "Get in the shower."

"This has been a total disaster!" Mary said. "I have to get downstairs to our guests..."

Rachel walked into the bathroom, turned on the shower, then came back and pushed Mary toward the bathroom door. After a couple of hesitant steps, Mary went along, took off her swimsuit, and climbed into the shower.

Then came a knock on the door. "It's Mom," Nacole said. "Can I come in?"

"Mary's in the shower right now," Rachel said. "Give her a few minutes."

"Is she OK?"

"Yeah, she's shaken up, but she's OK," Rachel said. "We'll be downstairs in a few minutes."

"We'll see you in a few minutes, then."

Rachel heard Mary crying in the shower. She slowly opened the door. "Are you going to be OK?" Rachel asked.

"I will be fine," Mary said.

"I don't know what to say," Rachel said.

"That's OK, you have already said enough," Mary smiled.

Rachel borrowed some of Mary's clothes, and the two friends quickly got dressed. Mary spent a little more time in the bathroom, using the supplies her mom had placed there quietly, expecting them to be used sooner or later. It turned out to be sooner.

Mary and Rachel went downstairs, where Jimmy and Nacole were waiting.

"Where is everybody?" Mary finally asked.

"We figured that after everything that happened, it probably was best to call it a day and send everyone home," Jimmy said. "The wind made a real mess out there and destroyed all the food. And I don't know what happened in the pool — maybe some strange reaction with the pool chemicals. I don't know. But nobody's going in there until we get it figured out."

Mary slumped onto the couch and started crying. Jimmy sat next to her, and she cried into his shoulder. Finally, still shaking, she looked at her dad and said, "I don't know how I'm going to be able to show my face at the Academy after what happened. All the kids laughing and staring at me, and the storm and everything."

Nacole sat down on the other side of Mary and took her daughter's face in her hands. "You're going to go to school Monday morning like nothing happened, young lady," Nacole said. "And if they laugh at you, just ignore them and hold your head high."

"That's easy for you to say, Mom."

"You can't quit after a week," Nacole said. "We moved down here so you wouldn't have to go to that terrible school your father and I went to. The Academy is the best school around, and you're going to get through this. Understand, young lady?"

Mary hated it when her mother called her "young lady." She sniffled. "OK, Mom. Just please don't yell at me."

Nacole smiled. She got it. Jimmy got it, too.

"But what do I do if they start yelling 'Bloody Mary!' again at school?"

"They're not going to," Rachel piped up. "And if they do, I'll walk right up to them and punch 'em in the nose. We'll see who's bloody!" All four of them laughed.

"What a party," Mary finally said. She looked around. "Is there any food left?"

"I baked a cake, and we got some ice cream," Nacole said. "The burgers and hot dogs are all over the backyard, so anybody want cake and ice cream?"

"Let's make it a birthday party," Jimmy said. He fumbled around in the kitchen, spotted where they had stashed birthday candles, and put them on the cake. He lit them, and he, Rachel, and Nacole all sang "Happy Birthday" to Mary — even though her birthday wasn't until January.

"Well, as long as this is a birthday," Rachel said, excusing herself and running up the spiral stairs.

"Where's she going?" Mary asked. Nacole just patted her hand and told her to sit still. Rachel quickly reappeared, lugging her backpack. She reached into it and pulled out a package in a department store gift bag.

"I would have wrapped it, but I wasn't sure when I would be giving it to you," Rachel said. "Now seems as good a time as any."

Mary looked around at her parents and pulled out a box from the bag.

"Open the lid," Rachel prompted. Mary did, and the gift began playing music—a very special song for Mary and Rachel.

"A music box!" Mary squealed. "But how…?"

"They just programmed it at the gift store at the mall," Rachel said. They both knew it was the song they heard on their second day together, and it was "their song."

Mary was crying again, this time from happiness. Jimmy took Nacole's hand, and they slipped out of the room.

"Has your day gotten better now, Mary?" Rachel asked.

Mary just nodded. This roller coaster of a day had been too much. Rachel leaned in, opened up the music box lid, smiled broadly, picked up her backpack, and slipped out the door. As she left, Mary ran upstairs, looked out the window, and saw Rachel go into her house. Mary put the music box on the dresser, opened it again, and let the song play through.

Finally, she went downstairs. Nacole was sitting alone at the marble kitchen counter. Jimmy had gone to bed early.

"Mom," Mary asked very quietly, "what really happened today?"

Nacole put her arm around her daughter.

"Sometimes strange things just come together," Nacole said. "That was a terrible, freak windstorm. That's all."

"But why did the pool water turn red?" Mary asked.

"That has to have been some reaction with the pool chemicals," Nacole said. "I didn't do real well in high school chemistry, so I can't really explain that."

"This has to have been the worst party ever," Mary wailed.

Nacole grimaced. No, she'd been to a worse party, long ago.

"Yeah, a windstorm, a chemical reaction, and rude guests," Nacole sighed. "But it could have been worse. It wasn't a tornado, nobody got hurt, and everybody went home safely."

"I guess you're right," Mary said, blinking back tears. "But it was supposed to be fun, and it wasn't much fun at all!"

Nacole just shook her head. "Why don't you go to bed, get some sleep, and it will look better in the morning."

"You're right, Mom," Mary said. "I love you. See you tomorrow."

"Tomorrow will be better," Nacole said. "I love you." She kissed her daughter goodnight, and Mary climbed up the spiral staircase.

Mary walked into her room, stared at the new mirror, and saw the bags under her eyes. She heard a sound outside on the

94

patio and looked down toward the pool. Her mother was next to the pool, and while Mary watched, Nacole reached down into the pool. She stood up and seemed to be holding something as she walked into the house.

"What's she got?" Mary asked herself. She shrugged, closed the curtains, and went to bed.

She fell asleep quickly, and then came the dream. She didn't want the dream, but she couldn't stop it. Her body twitched, she flipped from side to side, but she knew what was coming, and she couldn't stop it.

"Who will remember everything?" the voice said.

"Grace?" Mary mumbled. "What about my dad?"

"Don't go in the lake…"

Mary sat bolt upright in bed, her eyes wide with fear, her body covered with sweat, her heart pounding. She looked around. Nothing was out of place. It was just her room.

Mary lay back down slowly and cried herself to sleep.

CHAPTER EIGHT

The alarm came much too early. Mary stumbled out of bed and into her bathroom. She was still tired, but she caught some good smells coming from the kitchen downstairs. Mary went down to find Nacole making scrambled eggs, sausage, and toast. It smelled delicious. The girl hugged her mother and sat down at the counter as Nacole served breakfast for the two of them.

"Mom," Mary finally said, "I saw you out by the pool last night after I'd gone upstairs. What were you doing?"

"Nothing," Nacole said, a little too quickly. "We're draining the pool. We'll be filling it back up and putting in new chemicals." Nacole smiled. "And this time, we'll be careful to follow the directions!"

Mary nodded, returning her smile. Maybe everything would be okay after all. "Mom," she said a little hesitantly, "can I tell you something?"

"Of course! You can tell me anything, Mary." Nacole looked her daughter straight in the eye. "I'm your mother."

"I've been having some bad dreams," Mary responded. "Like almost every night. And they're almost the same dream, every time."

"Well, that's kind of strange."

"I never had a bad dream in my life before," Mary continued, finding it almost impossible to stop now that she had started. "Then we moved here, and I started to have nightmares out of nowhere."

"Do you remember them? What were they about?"

"I… I can't forget them if that's what you mean. And not from a lack of trying. They're terrible." Mary shuddered. She looked at the floor and began chewing on her thumbnail. She sat silently, trying to pluck up the courage to recall and narrate them to her mother. The silence dragged on and on until Nacole finally broke it.

"Well, are you going to tell me?"

"It scares me. I'm not sure I want to talk about it now."

"I need to know, baby," Nacole urged her daughter gently. She was concerned about her mental health. Maybe the change had been too drastic for her to handle. Mary finally looked up, pulled her thumb out of her mouth, and took a deep breath.

"It's almost always the same thing. There's this girl. She comes walking out of the water. She's always wearing a blue skirt and a yellow top."

"She's what?" Nacole asked, the description catching her off guard.

"I'm always right there with her," Mary continued. "Sometimes she'll talk to me."

"Well, what does she say?" Nacole asked, curious to know. Her brow furrowed, and her body felt rigid as she waited for an answer.

"Mom, she knows my name," Mary said. "She talks to me all the time."

"What else?"

"We're always standing on a beach somewhere. It's dark. There are people on the beach, and they're on fire. Some of them are dead. Some of them aren't. They're still screaming."

Nacole tried to keep herself calm and her expression neutral. If her daughter knew how horrifying her story was to Nacole, she'd be scarred for life. How could this be?

"And the woman," Mary continued, feeling the words come out like vomit, "she tells me she's my aunt."

Unbeknownst to Mary, Nacole began chewing on her own thumbnail in the same fashion that Mary had just been doing.

"The worst one though, is where she walked over to two burning bodies and said to me that one was her mother and the other was my father. She then looks right at me and says, 'Your mother is lying to you. You have the power to find the truth, and you won't have to take any crap from anyone ever again.' She told me her name was Grace."

Nacole was desperately trying to control her ragged breathing. She was failing. Mary didn't seem to notice; she was caught in her own terror as she recalled her dreams. "I know that dream has to be a lie. I don't have an Aunt Grace, and Dad's right outside draining the pool!" She turned to look at her mother, who was shaking uncontrollably.

Nacole tried to stop shaking but failed just as badly as she'd tried to stop her ragged breathing. She looked away from her daughter and said nothing. Her worst fear was coming to life, and she didn't know what to tell Mary. Up until now, she had been praying and hoping that she would never find out the truth.

Mary was confused. "Mom? Are you okay?"

Why was Mom acting like this? She was sure her mother would straight-up console her, not freak out like this. She was supposed to tell her that a dream was just a dream and there was no truth to it. But her reaction was saying the complete opposite. Was Mom hiding some kind of lie from me? What was going on here? All this weirdness! The broken mirror. The blood-red pool. The sudden windstorm. And now this.

"What is wrong? Answer me!" Mary finally said. "You look like you've seen a ghost!" Nacole blinked away tears.

"Just trying not to yawn, honey," Nacole said unconvincingly. "It's making my eyes water."

"Really? Are you sure that's it? Is there something you need to tell me? You know you can tell me anything, right? I mean, that's what you told me anyways." Mary gave her mother a look that almost made it seem like she was the mother talking to Nacole.

Nacole knew she needed to try to get it together. Her worst-case scenario was happening. She had hoped that all this would have just gone away, but here it was, right in front of her. She found it very difficult to look at her daughter.

"Mom!" Mary was getting a little upset. "You've got to tell me! You know something, don't you? The windstorm... the pool turning red. Mom, is there something wrong with me? Tell me!" Mary began to cry.

The older woman stepped away from the counter she had been leaning on for support and tried to put her arms around Mary, but Mary pushed her away. Mary stepped back.

"I've got to go," she said, turned, and walked out of the house.

Nacole broke down, sobbing like she knew that Mary would be now that she failed at reassuring her.

Finally, she pulled herself together. She looked at her purse lying on the marble countertop. She still had the sample of the pool water. Maybe she could get some answers. With at least some type of information, she could calm Mary down and tell her as much as she needed to know. Nacole wasn't sure she wanted the answers of the test, but she knew she had to get them. Damn it, she was the parent here!

CHAPTER NINE

Monday morning came, and things were not well between mother and daughter. They had spent the weekend avoiding each other, and this morning was no different. Mary had spent the entire Sunday wandering around alone with her thoughts, but she hadn't made any progress figuring things out. She'd come home late Sunday and quietly went to bed. Monday morning, she just grabbed a Pop-Tart before anyone else was up and stood outside for the school bus.

Nacole saw her daughter outside in the morning and decided it was best to leave things be. At least the girl was safe. After the bus picked up the neighborhood kids, Nacole drove to work to avoid an awkward encounter with her daughter.

Before she got to her office at the medical center, she had an important stop to make. She popped into the lab to see her friend Jones.

"Hey, Jones! How are you doing?"

"Hey, Nacole! Pretty good. What's up?"

"I need a favor," Nacole said. "I need you to analyze this pool water for me."

Jones was a skinny, slightly disheveled man, and looked too small for his white lab coat. He looked at the bottle Nacole had handed him, unscrewed the lid, and took a sniff.

"This doesn't smell like pool water to me," he said. "It sure doesn't look like pool water either."

"I know. That's why I want you to analyze it for me and tell me what's going on."

"Always happy to help you, Nacole." Jones looked at the bottle skeptically. "This should be easy. I'll have a report for you by the end of the day."

Nacole tried to concentrate on her work but found it difficult. She was anxiously waiting for the results to come back. Finally, just before four o'clock, her phone rang. It was Jones.

"I've got the test results. But you better come down to the lab to get them. I'm not comfortable talking about it over the phone."

That's not what she wanted to hear, but it was no worse than what she feared. She hurried down to the lab at the other end of the big medical facility where she worked. Jones was waiting for her.

"You're sure that came out of your pool?" Jones asked. "Because that's not pool water. I put it under the microscope, and this is blood."

Nacole swallowed hard. Jones continued. "Well, I figured since I was doing this, I might as well continue. I ran a DNA test on it. I figured someone was playing a prank or something. You know, using something like pig or steer blood."

"…And? Is it? Pig's blood?"

"Nope. This is 100 percent human blood. You sure this came out of your pool?"

Nacole nodded. Her knees were weak.

"Is there more of it out there?" Jones asked.

"No," Nacole replied curtly. "My husband drained the pool yesterday, and we're filling it up today with fresh water. We had to do something. As you can imagine... our daughter was pretty scared."

"Too bad," Jones said finally. "I would have liked to have my own sample. But anyway, I sequenced the DNA, and it doesn't match anything in the database here. Not yet anyway. But I'll let you know if something does come up." He smiled, unnervingly. He looked excited, and perhaps he was. His boring day had gotten interesting, even if just fleetingly. "It's definitely human, though."

"Yeah, well, thanks, Jones. I appreciate it." Nacole turned and hurried out of the building and straight home. She didn't want to know whose blood that was. She wanted everything to be normal, and she wanted to forget this ever happened. If only she could drain her brain of the memory of that day. Still… one problem at a time.

CHAPTER TEN

The whispering started on the bus. Mary and Rachel sat, as usual, at the back. As students piled in, they stared as they walked to their seats, then craned their necks to look at Mary and Rachel.

"Don't pay any attention to them, Mary," Rachel said.

Mary tried not to, but it was hard not to see them, hard not to get angry. And the stares continued after the school day started.

"They're making me angry," Mary muttered to Rachel in her first-hour class. "Who's laughing behind us?"

"It's Eric," Rachel whispered.

"I hate him," Mary said very quietly. Her eyes hardened. Her face turned hard as stone as she looked into the Darkness.

"Mary, are you OK?" Rachel asked.

"I'm… just… fine," Mary said, squeezing her notebook so hard her fingers turned white. "I'm… just… fine."

Behind her, someone's hand went up. "Yes, Eric," Mr. Thacker, the teacher, said.

"May I go to the restroom?" Eric chirped. Mr. Thacker rolled his eyes and motioned the boy out of the room. As he passed Mary's desk, she pointed the eraser end of her pencil at him and felt her anger boil. She quietly raised her hand.

"Sir, may I go to the girls' room?" she said.

Mr. Thacker sighed. "Anyone else?" No one answered. "Yes, Mary, go ahead. Your assignment will be waiting for you."

Mary quietly went out the door and down the hall. Everything was peaceful. She walked past the girls' room and pushed open the door to the boys' room. She went inside, and the hinges squeaked just a little as the door closed.

Eric flushed the urinal, zipped his pants, and turned around, surprised to see Mary in the boys' room.

"Hey, gorgeous," he said with a greasy smile. "What are you doing in here? The sign says 'boys.'"

"I know what it says," Mary said. "I just came here to have a little visit since you and I are such good friends. I mean, I must like you because I invited you to my party."

"Yeah, too bad the party went bad," Eric said. "Bloody Mary. Still mad at me?"

"No, not really," Mary lied. "Not anymore. But I will feel better when I get my revenge."

"Revenge? Whatcha gonna do, beat me up?"

"I haven't really thought about it," Mary said quietly. "No, I won't beat you up. I'll probably strangle you. You know, I could use that cloth towel dispenser."

The Academy's restrooms were equipped with old-fashioned towel machines that put a length of clean towel out for use, then rolled it back in as more was dispensed. But Mary had an idea. She smiled, then she stopped smiling as she looked once again into the Darkness.

"I think you need to leave now," Eric said quickly.

"Getting scared, Fat Boy?"

"Scared of who?" Eric tried to sound brave. "Scared of you? You've got to be kidding me!"

"This conversation has gotten boring. I think I'll kill you now," Mary said.

Eric pulled on the long roll of towel, and it didn't stop. It didn't pull the used towel back into the dispenser, either. Dozens of feet of towel simply rolled out onto the floor. Eric hit the machine with his fist, but the cloth kept rolling out.

Mary gazed more deeply into the Darkness. She was learning how to do this now. It wasn't hard, really. The towels on the floor began to writhe like a white cotton snake and quickly wrapped themselves around the young boy.

He couldn't move his arms. More cloth wrapped his face. He tried to scream, but his mouth was gagged with the cotton. More cloth twisted around his ankles, and he fell to the tile floor with a thud, hitting his head. Now the towels rolled themselves into a tight, white rope and wrapped around his neck once, twice, three times. It didn't take long for Eric to stop twitching.

In seconds, the takeup reel of the towel dispenser began to whir, pulling the used towel back up into the machine. Mary smiled. No, that wasn't hard at all, she thought.

She stepped to the door, looked both ways, and saw the hall was empty. She stepped out, and the door squeaked as it closed.

Mary slipped into the classroom and sat down next to Rachel.

"Where have you been?" Rachel hissed. "You've been gone almost half an hour!"

"I went to the bathroom," Mary said smoothly. "Remember, I'm on my period, and I'm not real good at that stuff yet."

Rachel just stared, then went back to working on the assignment.

Mr. Thacker realized that Mary had been gone a long time, and that Eric had been gone even longer. What was that boy up to?

"Keep working, people," Mr. Thacker said. "I'll be right back." Ninth-grade boys, he thought. Always testing the limits.

"Where is Eric?" Rachel asked Mary.

"I dunno," Mary said. "Maybe the fat boy fell in and plugged up the toilet. I don't really care."

"I don't like him anyway," Mary said.

Suddenly, the Academy's bells began to ring. The principal came on the public address system, saying, "Lockdown. Lockdown. All classrooms go to lockdown. Lockdown. Lockdown."

One of the school secretaries came into the classroom and quickly locked the door behind her. Her eyes were wide. The ninth-graders gathered around her.

"Mrs. Van Houten, what's going on? Is this an active shooter?" somebody asked.

"We don't know," the middle-aged woman said. "All we know is that Mr. Thacker found a student's body in the boys' restroom."

The class gasped as one. Eric! It had to be him!

Rachel looked at Mary, who was sitting quietly in her seat. "Mary?" Rachel said. "You did this, didn't you?"

"How could I? He was in the boys' room. I'm not allowed in there," Mary said, with just a hint of a smile. "But if he's really dead, I'm not sad."

"How can you say that?" Rachel demanded. "You're acting really funny, Mary. You're scaring me."

"You have nothing to be afraid of, Rachel," Mary said calmly. "But after what he did to me at the party, well, I don't really care."

"I can't believe you said that," Rachel said.

The classroom's telephone rang, and Mrs. Van Houten answered it. She nodded several times and looked very serious. Finally, she hung up and spoke to the students.

"OK, class, here's what's going on," she said. "There's a police SWAT team on-site, and they will be going through the school, room by room, to make sure everyone's OK. Before they get here, they want me to take roll and make sure everyone but Eric…" At that point, she broke down. Most of the girls began crying too, and even some of the boys. Mary sat quietly, her hands in her lap, a faraway look in her eyes.

"You're still scaring me," Rachel whispered.

Mrs. Van Houten finally pulled herself together, found the class gradebook, and called the roll. All but one was present, and she called that in. Shortly after that, a key grated in the door, and the school principal, accompanied by four heavily armed, heavily armored police officers with helmets and automatic rifles, stomped into the room.

Mary tried not to giggle at the way the officers looked. All she could think of were bug-eyed monsters from bad, old science fiction movies.

"We're going to keep the lockdown going for a little while longer," the principal said. "We've accounted for everybody, and there's just the one, um, casualty. We'll be sending everybody home, but this class is the one where the, uh, casualty came from, so we'll have to pay particularly close attention to you guys."

"There are TV cameras outside in front, so we'll be sending you out the back of the school to keep you safe," the principal said. "I've already talked to the local news this morning, and they seemed disappointed there wasn't any gunfire." He sighed. "You guys stay right here with Mrs. Van Houten. Mr. Thacker is talking to the response team, and we'll be talking to all of you. Just relax, if you can."

He looked around and spotted Mary. "Mary, Mr. Thacker said you went to the restroom right after Eric did," the principal said. "Would you come with me? Everybody else, sit tight. You'll get your turn."

Mary turned to Rachel with a pleading look, but Rachel couldn't do anything. The principal led Mary out the door, followed by the four bug-eyed monsters with guns. They went into a conference room next to the main office, where a half-dozen people sat around a table, looking concerned.

A sharply dressed woman introduced herself and the other people in the room. Mary didn't remember any of the names, but she heard words like "trauma psychologist," "grief counselor," and "investigator." That applied to a rumpled-looking man, who motioned Mary to sit down.

"You're Mary, right?" he asked. He pulled what looked like a mobile device from inside his suit jacket, set it on the table, and pushed a button. "You're Mary, right?"

She nodded. "Please speak up," he said.

"Yes, I'm Mary," she finally said.

"We need to ask a few questions, and we're starting with you because Mr. Thacker told us that both you and Eric went to the restroom about the same time this morning."

"Well, I don't think he had the same problem I did," Mary said, catching the eye of the well-dressed woman. "I'm on my period."

The rumpled man seemed to deflate a little. "I, uh, see," he stammered. "Um, OK, did you see anything out of the ordinary in the hallway this morning?"

"No, sir," she said. "The hallways were empty. Everybody was in class."

"You didn't hear anything?" the rumpled man asked. "No screaming? No yelling?"

"No, sir," Mary said. "I just had to take care of things. When I did, I came back to class. Then all this craziness started."

The well-dressed woman interrupted. "Mary, are you feeling OK? Are you all right?"

"Just some cramps," Mary said. "Really, I'm OK. Are there really TV cameras outside?"

"There are," the woman said. "Don't worry about them." She handed Mary a photocopied list of phone numbers and websites where she could call or go if she needed help. The rumpled man handed her a business card. Yep, he was a cop.

"Call me if you remember anything," he said. "You can go back to your classroom."

"No problem, um," Mary fumbled with the business card, "Sgt. Stadeski." She got up and left. She didn't see the SWAT team people in the hall anymore.

Mary came back into the classroom and sat down at her desk. Most of the students were streaming live coverage of "The Incident at the Academy" on their phones, posting what they knew and a lot of what they didn't know online.

"What did they want to know?" Rachel asked.

"They just asked if I'd seen anything and if I was doing OK," Mary said. "I told them I hadn't seen anything and that I'm doing fine except I've got cramps."

"You didn't see anything?" Rachel said.

"No."

"Why don't I believe you?" Rachel shot back.

"I don't care if you believe me or not," Mary said. "Now you're making me mad. You're calling me a liar. I don't like that."

"I don't know," Rachel said. "It just seems weird. He left, you left, you hate his guts, you came back and he didn't. And now he's dead. And it's all over the TV."

"Sucks to be him, doesn't it?" Mary said. Rachel sighed deeply.

The girls heard the public address system begin scratching as it turned on. The principal came on and rehashed in general terms what was going on, offered counseling for those who felt they would need it, and announced that school would be dismissed early. Mr. Thacker, his face still pale and haggard, came back to the classroom. He looked as if he might have been crying.

"We'll probably have a memorial for poor Eric," he sputtered. "It will be announced. Right now, the buses will be arriving. Head home, stay safe."

Rachel and Mary exchanged looks, picked up their books, and headed for the bus. They found their seat in the back.

"So should we go to the vigil?" Rachel asked.

"I don't think that would be smart," Mary said. "I might start laughing and clapping."

"You're mean."

"He made me mad. I won't forget."

"You want me to come over later?" Rachel asked.

"Yeah. We can just chill in my room for a while." The two girls reached their houses and went to their doors.

Rachel turned around, watching her best friend walk into her house. She was concerned about the way Mary was acting. She knew there was something more going on with Mary than what she was telling her.

Mary's house was empty. Her mom was at work, as well as her dad. Mary climbed the spiral staircase, finally reaching her room, and went into the bathroom. She decided she just wanted a nice hot bath and some cookies.

Mary started running the water into the tub that would carry any of her worries away. She ran downstairs, grabbed a few chocolate chip cookies from the jar that was sitting on the Italian marble countertop, and ran back upstairs. The water that was cascading into the tub was extra warm to the touch, and steam was coming off of it and floating toward the ceiling. Mary, watching the water flowing into the tub, slid out of her clothes and climbed into the water, first dipping her toe in and then following with the rest of her body. She couldn't help but think to herself just how amazing the water felt as she slowly lowered herself into the oasis. Mary continued to let her body relax into the water and eventually she was submerged completely, except for her face.

But then it happened—the slam of a car door that effectively broke her sense of zen, causing Mary to swear.

"You have got to be kidding me! Really, Mom?" she said just above a whisper.

"Mary… are you home?" Nacole yelled from the downstairs entry.

"Yes, Mom!" Mary called out. "I'll be down in just a minute." And then she quickly added, "Oh, and Mom… Rachel is supposed to be coming over for a little while, OK?"

"OK, honey, sounds good!" Nacole shouted back.

Mary rushed to dry off and put her clothes on. Afterward, she climbed down the stairs, and just as she reached the bottom, there was a knock at the door.

"I'll get it," Nacole said, and as she opened the door, there was Rachel standing in the midst. "Oh, hey, Rachel, come on in and make yourself at home."

"Mom, Rachel and I are going up to my room to just chill for a while."

"OK, Mary, no prob. So, do you girls have anything to tell me before you head up to the room about what happened today?"

Both girls just looked at each other and shrugged.

Nacole felt obligated to explain her reason for coming home early.

"The reason I came home early is that your principal called me at work to tell me that one of your classmates had died at school and therefore classes were dismissed early for the day. I saw some of it on television; however, there weren't a lot of details yet."

Mary shrugged her shoulders and said, "Yeah... Eric went into the bathroom at school and died, and that was about it, really."

"What?" Nacole shouted. "Eric? The same Eric who was here at the pool party? The rude rat kid?"

"Yeah," Mary said. "Same kid."

Nacole looked sharply at her daughter. She had a bad feeling about this.

"What killed him?" Nacole asked.

"I dunno," Mary said. "Maybe he, like, had an undiagnosed heart condition, like that kid in the state basketball championship game last spring who scored the winning basket and died right there."

Mary knew more about this than she was letting on, Nacole thought. But she didn't want to go there. Not now. Not ever.

"Have they said anything at the school?" Nacole said.

"Nope."

"Maybe they've got something on the news," Nacole said. She walked over to the big-screen TV in the living room and turned on one of the local stations. A picture of the Academy was on the screen, along with a chyron that said "LIVE!" and another that read, "SOON: PRESS CONFERENCE ON ACADEMY DEATH."

"Well, maybe they'll say something here," Nacole said. "Have you girls had lunch?"

"I had a couple of cookies," Mary said.

"Stay for lunch, Rachel," Nacole said. "I'll make some tomato soup and sandwiches while we wait for the press conference."

Nacole went into the kitchen to start cooking. "Call me if they start talking, OK?"

It didn't take long before Sheriff Dewayne Jackson lumbered up to the podium set up in front of the cameras on the Academy's front lawn.

"I have a statement, and then I'll take questions," Jackson said, his jowls flopping as he spoke, and his "Smokey Bear" hat casting an unfortunate shadow across his face, making him look threatening.

"Mom!" Mary called. "They're starting!"

Nacole came out of the kitchen, wiping her hands.

"We had a tragic event here at the Academy today," Jackson said, almost as if he were giving a campaign speech. "A little boy was found expired in a restroom."

"Expired?" Mary giggled. "Like a carton of milk? Did he go sour?"

"Shh!" both Nacole and Rachel said at once.

"We have a tentative identification on the fourteen-year-old," Jackson said.

"Tentative? You know it's Eric!" Mary shot back at the TV.

"But we won't be releasing the name of the young man until his next of kin have been notified. Now, let me walk you through the timeline. At 8:48 a.m. this date..."

Jackson squinted down at a paper in front of him, then put on a pair of dark-rimmed glasses that made him look like a bulldog with goggles. "At 8:48 a.m., Central Dispatch received a 911 call from the academy pertaining to a non-responsive student in the downstairs boys' room. At 8:49 a.m., an emergency medical services ambulance was dispatched. EMS arrived at 9:02 and determined the student appeared to be deceased."

"Like, he was dead," Mary said. This time, she just got dirty looks from her friend and her mother.

"EMS reported no visible trauma," the sheriff continued, "but in an abundance of caution, I ordered the activation of the county Special Weapons and Tactics Team to ensure that if the student's passing was the result of an act of violence, the other students would be protected."

Mary opened her mouth but decided not to say anything. She wondered how hard it might be to bend the barrels of the rifles the SWAT team members had been carrying that morning. Just a thought.

"After sweeping the school..." the sheriff rambled on.

"You found dust bunnies but no more bodies?" Mary said brightly. Rachel just rolled her eyes.

"...law enforcement determined that no further threat existed and all other students were accounted for. We immediately began our investigation. The Academy called in its emergency response team of counselors and other experts," Jackson said, pulling himself fully erect before the microphones and cameras. "The young man's remains have been transported to Memorial Hospital for an autopsy and formal identification. We don't know the cause of death. The autopsy will determine that. Any questions?"

The gaggle of reporters all shouted at the sheriff. One asked when the Academy would be open again. Jackson looked around, a little lost, then spotted the principal in the crowd. Jackson motioned him before the cameras.

"Because of the traumatic nature of the event today," he said, "and to provide Sheriff Jackson and his team full access in case they need it, school will be canceled for the rest of the week."

"Yippee!" Mary shouted.

"That's just not nice," Rachel said. "The kid's dead."

"And I hated his guts after what he said," Mary said. "What's not to like? Eric's pushing up daisies and we get a week off from school. Is this what they mean by win-win? We win, and we win!"

Nacole shook her head. "How can you still hate him even after he's dead?"

"I will always hate him for what he did at the party," Mary said. "'Bloody Mary! Bloody Mary!' And the rest of the kids who joined in. Oooooooh! They'll get what's coming to them!"

"Remind me never to get you mad at me," Rachel said.

Nacole looked thoughtful, then went to the kitchen. She brought out bowls of soup and cold-cut sandwiches. When they were finished, Rachel said she'd have to go home so she could tell her mother what happened.

"I don't think I'll be able to come back today," Rachel said. "Mom will probably want to keep an eye on me, just to be Mom. I'll see you tomorrow, OK?"

CHAPTER ELEVEN

The next morning, Mary was still asleep as her mother
went out the door and got into her car. Nacole was about to close
the car door when she saw Rachel running across the street toward
her.

"Rachel," Nacole said, caught off guard. "You're up early
on a day off from school! What's going on?"

"I have to talk to you," Rachel said breathlessly. "About
Mary."

Nacole felt her insides scrunch up painfully. She already
knew where this was going, and she didn't like it. Not at all.
Nacole put on a pleasant smile.

"What about Mary?" she asked cautiously. "Is everything
OK between the two of you?"

"Yeah, we're fine," Rachel said. "She's my best, best friend
forever. And that's why I'm so worried about her."

Nacole climbed out of the car. She didn't want this to get
out of hand. "So, Rachel, why are you worried about Mary?"

"Since the pool party, she's just gotten... different."

"Different," Nacole repeated. *That's true,* she thought.
"What do you mean by that, Rachel?"

The girl hesitated. "I... I don't know, really," Rachel
answered. "It's hard to put into words, but things have just gotten...
weird."

That's putting it mildly, Nacole thought. But she just smiled at her daughter's best friend.

"Tell me more, Rachel," Nacole said once she realized that Rachel wasn't going to give any more than she did. She needed to find out how much this girl actually knew. How much did she figure out?

"Well... even before the pool party, I saw that the mirror was cracked in Mary's room. She told me how it cracked all by itself... I mean, OK, I guess that can happen. But then when the pool water turned red—"

"Oh, that?" Nacole interrupted. "Jimmy must not have mixed the pool chemicals right, and we had a strange reaction. When we drained the pool and filled it again, he made sure he followed the directions this time!"

Nacole knew she was on thin ice but told herself to just stick to the story. *Did I swear Jones to silence?* she wondered. Well, great. Now she had something else to worry about.

"And the windstorm," Rachel continued. "I talked to some of the other kids at school who weren't at the party, and no one heard or saw anything about a windstorm on Saturday afternoon except for the kids who were just here..."

Nacole just shrugged.

"And then there was Eric... Mary went right out the door after he left for the restroom. Both of them were gone for a long time. Mary came back, and she had this kind of—I don't know—this, like, crazy look on her face. No... not crazy. Not psycho... just, I guess... like satisfied. And Eric... he never came back."

Nacole looked away. She found that she couldn't look Rachel in the eyes.

"And then there was the press conference. The way Mary kept mouthing off during it... it was all really mean."

"Well, our sheriff isn't exactly a TV star," Nacole replied. "But why are you saying all this about Mary? What are you trying to get at? You can tell me, Rachel."

"I'm just telling you because I worry about her. And you're her mother. You are the only other person who won't judge her but always wish her well." Rachel felt her eyes misting up.

"Rachel, Rachel," Nacole said, noticing the tears. She grabbed one of her hands and patted it softly. "I understand that some of these things are crazy by themselves. But to put them together the way you seem to be suggesting... You're not one of those conspiracy theory people, are you?"

Rachel shook her head. "I guess it all could be a coincidence."

"That's right. Stop worrying. You've all been under a lot of stress and trauma. Mary just moved to a new school, a new house, a new neighborhood. You've just found out a kid you've probably known your whole life had just passed away—and so abruptly, too. It all piles up. It makes sense for you to look for answers as a way to find some certainty in this unpredictable time. But it's a coincidence," Nacole finished, smiling sweetly and continued rubbing her hand.

"I'm going to have to go to work," Nacole said suddenly. Rachel just nodded. "Why don't you go over and keep Mary company after she gets up today?"

Rachel brightened and nodded. "That's OK with you?"

"Sure," Nacole said, climbing into her car. She closed the door and started the engine. While pulling out, she said to herself, "I've got to see Jones first thing and make sure he doesn't say anything to anyone."

CHAPTER TWELVE

The whispering started almost as soon as classes resumed at the Academy. Mary thought that every kid at her high school and most of the faculty were giving her the side-eye as she walked the corridors. She could almost hear them saying, "Bloody Mary... Bloody Mary... Bloody Mary" in hushed whispers as she walked past.

Sometimes, she would look into the distance and see the Darkness. No, it wasn't time. Not yet. She could afford to be patient for a little while, but she knew her patience would run out.

And when that happened... well, she'd have to make sure Rachel didn't get hurt. But the way things looked right now, all those whisperers... she might not be able to control herself for much longer. Bloody Mary, indeed.

When school ended, she and Rachel rode home. Mary was very, very quiet.

"You're scaring me again, Mary," Rachel finally broke the silence.

"Am I?" Mary said, forcing a smile. "You don't have anything to be scared of." And she wasn't lying, because Rachel didn't. But those other kids better watch out.

At the bus stop, Mary told Rachel goodbye and said she would see her later. Mary spotted her mom's car in the driveway and told Rachel she needed to talk to her mom about something and that Rachel should come over after dinner. Rachel gave a mock pout but relented.

When Mary came into the house, it was filled with the marvelous scent of onions, garlic, and herbs being sautéed. That could only mean one thing: Mom was making something really special for dinner. That was too bad; what Mary had to say couldn't wait and would definitely ruin the mood.

"Hi, Mom!" Mary said as she walked into the kitchen.

"Hey, baby! You're home!" Nacole answered. "How was the first day back at school?"

"Hell."

"How?"

"All the whispering, 'Bloody Mary, Bloody Mary,' got old. And the glances. The whole school is in on it. I hate them. I hate them all so much."

"Should I call the principal?"

"No, Mom," Mary said. "He can't stop it even if he wanted to. But I can, and I will. But in due time."

"What do you mean by that?" Nacole asked loudly. No, no, not now, not ever.

"Mom, you and I have to talk. There's a lot you haven't told me. Maybe you've even lied to me."

"I've never lied to you."

"Oh, yeah?" Mary shot back. "What about the man you're married to, calling him my father? Isn't that a lie?"

"Mary..."

"My father's dead, and Jimmy adopted me. You never told me. And what about my Aunt Grace? How did she die? What are you hiding, Mom?"

Nacole's mouth moved, but nothing came out. She knew this day would come, but she hoped against hope that it wouldn't. Nacole reached over and turned off the flame and removed the pan from the stove. She turned to face her daughter, who wasn't done talking yet.

"I've seen it all in my dreams, Mom, and they're real. All those dead kids on the beach... my dead father... Aunt Grace. Is she your half-sister? And the Darkness. You know all about it, Mom, don't you? Don't you?"

"Mary, you need to understand... your father and I just wanted to protect you!"

"He's not even my real father! Stop lying to me!" Mary reached over and flipped the sauté pan full of butter, onions, and herbs, dumping it all over the floor. "I don't care about dinner. I don't care about you! I'm going to go lie down, and don't you dare bother me! If Rachel comes over, you can let her in, but otherwise,

NO ONE else. Not you, not Dad, or whoever he is. Just stay away from me!"

She ran up the spiral staircase and slammed the door of her room. Nacole picked up her phone and quickly texted Jimmy.

Mary knows everything. Call me. Urgent.

In seconds, the phone was ringing. It was Jimmy. "What do you mean, she knows everything?"

"Somehow, she knows about graduation night. She knows about Grace. We can't talk on the phone. Come home. Just come home."

"I'm on my way, Nacole." With that, he hung up.

Nacole was just finishing cleaning up the splatter from the pan when Jimmy's truck roared into the driveway. He ran through the patio door, kissed Nacole, and sat down. Jimmy could tell that Nacole had been crying.

"So... what does she know?" Jimmy finally asked.

"It seems like she knows everything, Jimmy. Graduation night. Grace. Powers. And how to use them. She even knew about Kent."

Jimmy swore. He never swore.

"And she told me Grace is my half-sister," Nacole continued.

"If she is, that's news to me."

"Me too," Jimmy agreed. "So... powers. You think Mary's behind all the weird stuff then?"

"Well, I mean... think about it, Jimmy." Nacole looked off to the side, as if she was afraid to make eye contact. "Remember the mirror in her room?"

"Yeah. I just figured... it was faulty, or something. Like there were stress fractures already in the mirror when we got it and just didn't notice it. I mean, the guys from the store were very apologetic and replaced it right away."

"Well, here's what I heard the day the mirror broke. Mary was trying on clothes, and they didn't fit, and she got mad and screamed. That's when I heard the sound of glass breaking. When I went upstairs later, all I saw was shattered glass bits everywhere and a hysterical Mary. She was freaked out and didn't know how it broke. But the next day, as you were taking it out, there were cracks all over the mirror, but it was still all in one piece."

"OK, so what does that mean?" Jimmy asked.

"It was more like pieces of a jigsaw puzzle joined back together. She couldn't have put them back together by hand. I saw the broken glass myself.

"And then there's the pool party. That windstorm that happened just here, but nowhere else. I checked. Everywhere else that day? Clear and listless."

"That's impossible. Weather can vary from place to place, but a windstorm only here?" Jimmy bit his lip in frustration.

"Impossible or not, it's true. And the pool turning red. You know what that was, right?"

"Bad chemicals?"

"No. It was blood, Jimmy."

"Well, yeah... Mary started her period in the pool, remember?"

"You don't get it. There was forty thousand gallons of it. All human. And all in our pool." Nacole shuddered.

"How do you know it was blood anyway?"

"I had Jones at the hospital test it. He confirmed it." Nacole told him the tale. Jimmy gasped. "And I swore him to secrecy."

"Good," Jimmy said.

"And the kid who died mysteriously at school last week? He's the mouthy little punk who started the 'Bloody Mary' thing."

"I wanted to punch him in the mouth... wait a second... you don't think... Mary did it, do you?" Jimmy looked sick to his stomach.

"I've been following the news," Nacole continued, not answering him directly. "The medical examiner says he died apparently of asphyxiation, but there wasn't a mark on his body. And Mary wasn't in the classroom when Eric died."

"Well, where was she?" Jimmy wondered aloud.

"She says she was in the girls' room dealing with her period."

"I'd hate to argue with that," Jimmy sighed.

"But here's the scariest part," Nacole said. "She says she knew what happened at the lake that night."

"How?"

"I don't know. But she described it just like it was. And she knows about Grace."

"How could she possibly know?" Jimmy asked. "I've never told her. Have you?"

"Of course not, Jimmy!"

"How do you think she knows?" Jimmy asked, pointing out the obvious.

"Well, Mary said she saw it all in a dream. Grace was there as well, and talked to her about it." Nacole started to cry.

"Grace is dead." Jimmy sounded more sure than he looked.

"And she knows that you adopted her and her biological dad is dead, dead on the beach on graduation night." Nacole was having a hard time keeping it all together.

"We promised we'd never tell her, so I know that she didn't get that info from anyone else. As far as the world's concerned, I'm her father and always would be." Jimmy looked shocked.

"Mary says it was Grace telling her all this, in the dream."

"Again, that's just not possible."

"Yeah, well... neither is what happened that night at the lake, Jimmy." At this, Nacole broke down completely and fell into Jimmy's arms.

Jimmy held his wife for a while as she cried and cried. After what felt like forever, she finally shuddered and pulled away ever so slightly.

"So, what's this about Grace being your half-sister?" Jimmy asked gently.

"I don't know," Nacole answered. "If she is, I've never been told by anyone."

"Your dad would know."

"Yes, he would," Nacole agreed, wiping her tears away. She picked up the phone and gave his line a ring. After another long eternity, he answered.

"Hey, Dad, it's Nacole." Her father refused to get caller ID, so she had to identify herself whenever she called. In the past, she thought it was quaint, but now she found it rather annoying.

"Sweetie!" Wayne said way too loudly. "How are you? Jimmy? Mary? Is everything OK?"

"It's been a rough week," Nacole said, afraid to get into too much and risk crying again. "You've been seeing what's going on with Mary's school on the news, right?"

"Yes, that's just terrible. I've been meaning to call. Is that what's on your mind, to tell me what a terrible father and grandfather I've been?"

Nacole wasn't sure what that meant, so she ignored it. "Look, Dad, I've got a question about your past I need an answer for. Did you know a girl named Elizabeth in high school?"

"Wow, I haven't thought about her in years, but yes. She died in the gas explosion down by the lake, right?"

"Yes, she did. But did you know her in high school?"

"Yes, as a matter of fact," Wayne said. "We dated a little bit, and then she invited me up to her room. It was quite creepy. Candles and black curtains and all that. It was a little romantic, but mostly creepy."

"So... did you have sex with her?"

"I mean, I'm a red-blooded American, and she was willing, so..."

"Did you use protection?"

"She told me she was on the pill. I don't know if she lied or told the truth," the older man said. "But after that, I never went back. It was too creepy."

"And you were dating Mom around the same time, right?"

"Well, yeah... that too. Anyway, Elizabeth just disappeared right after graduation."

"When you and Mom graduated, she was pregnant with me, right?" Nacole asked carefully. The next few sentences might be tense.

"Yeah. It was like that old song, 'two American kids, doing the best they can,' right?" her father said, laughing. So far, so good.

"I think you got Elizabeth knocked up, too," Nacole said quietly.

"Hey, she never told me, and if she was, well, she might have been crazy and weird, but she was cool enough to go away." Her father wasn't laughing anymore.

"But if she were, the baby would be my half-sister, right?" Nacole realized she was thinking out loud but didn't know what else to say.

"Lot of speculation there, sweetie," her dad said. "But even if she were, I don't think it was mine. She would have told me."

"How do you know that?" Nacole wondered.

"Because we always had money, and she would have wanted it," the older man said matter-of-factly. "Not that she would have an easy time getting it."

"Maybe, maybe not. Hey, you remember that girl Grace from high school, who went crazy at graduation and caused all that devastation? The one who threw fireballs—"

"Sweetie," her dad interrupted, "don't tell me you're thinking of that day again. That was a gas leak, and you know it. You and Jimmy spent weeks in the loony bin getting your heads straightened out, remember? You imagined all that. It never happened like you thought. Got it?"

"Dad, Grace had powers," Nacole said, firmly.

"Grace died," her father said. "And there is no such thing as 'powers.'"

"And if Mary is related to her, she could have the powers too, right?"

"Don't be bringing my granddaughter into this. You're talking crazy, Nacole. Is Jimmy there? Let me talk to him." Nacole handed her husband the phone.

"Wayne?" Jimmy said.

"Listen, Jimmy, take care of your wife. I think she's cracking up again. I remember how fragile the two of you were after the explosion. Keep an eye on her, buddy, OK?"

"Wayne, we both saw what we saw. She's not crazy," Jimmy said. "And some weird stuff has started happening around here, and we're trying to get to the bottom of it. Believe your daughter, Wayne. I know it sounds crazy, but it's true. Something is up with your granddaughter too."

"There's nothing wrong with my granddaughter," Wayne spluttered, frustrated. "But it sounds like her parents have both gone off the deep end!"

"Wayne," Jimmy persisted, "I saw everything graduation night. No one ever believed us. But I saw Grace touch Nacole's stomach and tell her she was going to have a very special little girl. Now I'm afraid of what that means, but I can tell you this. No one has ever told her that I'm not her biological father. I'm sure of that. And now she knows, somehow. Listen, why don't you come over to the new place? You haven't visited yet, right? I'll walk you through everything that has happened."

"Jimmy, you're a good kid," Wayne said. "I do want to see that house sometime when you're all well. But if you're going to talk crazy, I'd rather stay away. So listen, sport; I'll see if I can find that number for that psychiatrist who did you and Nacole so much good back then. But no more crazy talk about fireballs and powers. That's my granddaughter you're talking about, and I don't want her getting sucked into all that madness." Wayne hung up quickly, before Jimmy could say anything back. Jimmy clicked the phone off and handed it back to his wife.

"Blood in the pool. The broken mirror. That weird windstorm. And maybe even a dead kid. Nacole, I feel it. And you know it too. We're on our own again."

CHAPTER THIRTEEN

The Academy's school bus came down the road at the unusual hour of 10:30 a.m. The school was dismissed early after a construction crew hit a major water main, sending a spectacular geyser out of the hole they were digging. The water main wasn't supposed to be anywhere near the project, but there it was. The Academy and several blocks around it would have no water until further notice.

Rachel and Mary didn't care. They'd become even closer as time passed. Occasional whispers of "Bloody Mary" still surfaced, but no one said anything to Mary's face.

"Want to go swimming?" Mary asked Rachel as they left the bus.

"When?"

"As soon as you can grab your swimsuit," Mary smiled.

"You're on!"

Rachel ran across the road to her house. Her mother's car was in the driveway, but Nacole's car and Jimmy's truck weren't around. Mary let herself in, went to the kitchen, and found bread, cold cuts, and a family-sized bag of potato chips to munch on.

She slathered the meat with mayonnaise, put a handful of chips on her plate, and cracked open a bottle of cold water. Mary turned on the big-screen TV in the breakfast nook, where someone dressed as a pickle was attempting to win a new car.

"Hmmmm... a pickle would be good." She looked into the refrigerator but didn't see any pickle jars. She looked under the counter where her mother stored canned goods but found no pickles there either. The pickle on TV shrieked with joy. Apparently, she'd won the car.

"Where's Rachel?" Mary wondered out loud. She picked up her phone and sent her a text: *Where r u?* Mary went back to looking for her pickles.

Ten minutes later, she realized Rachel hadn't replied. Mary texted her again. Nothing. She made a voice call. "Hi, it's Rachel. I'm either really busy or I don't recognize your caller ID, so I'm going to let your call go to voicemail. Always text first! Leave a message!"

Mary didn't leave a message. She was really worried now. She shot off a quick text to Rachel's mom.

Rachel over there? It's Mary.

The older woman responded immediately. *No. She's at your house, isn't she?*

A cold chill struck Mary as she saw the text on the screen. *No.*

The phone rang immediately, and Mary picked up. It was Rachel's mom.

"What do you mean... she's not at your house?" the woman asked, sounding upset. "I sent her out the door almost a half-hour ago."

"She's not here!"

"I'll be right over." Rachel's mom hung up.

Rachel's mom, Sue, could have been an older version of her daughter. She was a little shorter than average, dark-haired, with lively eyes. But the woman standing outside Mary's front door wasn't smiling today.

"Are you telling me that my daughter disappeared between there"—pointing to her own house across the way—"and here?" Sue asked.

"Wait... do you really think... she disappeared?" Mary asked, suddenly realizing that that was exactly what happened.

"I watched her go out the door," Sue said, "and she's not here. So..."

"Maybe she's playing games?" Mary suggested. "I was in the kitchen. Rachel's over here so much she just comes in the front door. Come on upstairs. Let's look in my room."

Sue and Mary climbed the spiral stairs. The room was empty. So was the bathroom.

"I see why she likes to come over here," Sue said, admiring her daughter's best friend's room.

Mary opened the curtains. She had learned to keep them closed because the guy next door—"Creepy John," she had begun thinking of him—kept looking out his window in the direction of her house.

Mary looked around outside, then looked down at the pool. She screamed and almost collapsed. Sue rushed to the window, caught the girl, and then looked down at the pool.

There, in the pool, was a slender young girl in an Academy uniform, at the bottom of the pool and not moving. It had to be Rachel.

"Rachel!" Sue and Mary screamed together.

Both bolted for the bedroom door, with Sue slightly ahead of Mary on the staircase. Mary almost ran through the glass patio door but realized in time that it was closed and opened the door to get through. Sue got to the edge of the pool and dove straight in. Her long-forgotten Girl Scout lifeguard training kicked in, and she plucked Rachel off the bottom and brought her to the surface.

"Help me get her into the shallow end!" Sue cried out. Mary pulled her friend down to where Sue could stand up. "Get in here and hold her head up! I'm going to give her rescue breathing."

She put her mouth on her daughter's mouth and began giving her five quick breaths... but something was wrong. Those breaths weren't going anywhere. A quick pulse check. No. No. No! She had to have a pulse! Check again. No pulse. This couldn't be happening!

"Mary!" Sue called out. "Call 911, now!"

Mary realized she'd climbed into the pool with her phone, but she didn't need to worry, as it worked fine. She dialed 911.

"Eastern Regional Dispatch," the bored-sounding operator answered. "What's the nature of your emergency?"

"My best friend Rachel was at the bottom of my pool," Mary managed to get out. "She's not breathing. I think she's drowned!"

"Give me your address, please." He didn't sound bored anymore.

Mary did, and it matched the geolocation information on the dispatcher's screen. That didn't always happen, so the dispatcher breathed a sigh of relief. He quickly zoomed out, hit a couple of keys, and the nearest police, rescue, and ambulance units appeared on his screen. This was not good; it would take at least 12 minutes for a rescue unit to get to their isolated location. But a police unit was only a couple of miles away. The dispatcher clicked on the police car, the rescue unit, another police car a few miles farther away, and the ambulance, which was 20-plus minutes away at the Medical Center.

"Is she breathing?" the dispatcher asked.

"No."

"Does she have a pulse?"

"I don't know," Mary said. She was shaking hard.

"Sue, does she have a pulse?"

"I can't find one!" the girl's mother cried, desperately trying to get her daughter to breathe again.

"Is there somebody there who can give her CPR?" the dispatcher asked as he rapidly gave dispatching instructions to the responding units.

"Can you give CPR?" Mary asked Sue.

"I can, but not in the water like this. Help me get her on the deck!"

Mary put the phone down, and the dispatcher heard her jump into the water. This part of the pool was only three feet deep, so as Sue supported Rachel's head, Mary boosted the ninth grader up onto the concrete deck. Sue quickly leaped from the water and began applying chest compressions on the girl. Mary picked up the phone.

"OK, sorry," she gasped. "I'm back. Rachel's mom seems to know how to do this."

"Help is on the way," the dispatcher said. He did his best to remain calm but felt his adrenaline coursing through his bloodstream. "When the first responders get there, can they get to the pool where you guys are?"

Mary looked around. For the first time, she noticed that the gate through the pool fence was wide open. *That's weird,* Mary thought. *Rachel knows better than that. Some little kid could wander in and drown,* but then realized how insane her thinking was. *Rachel was drowning right now. Rachel sure wasn't a little kid.*

She heard a single siren off in the distance. "Please hurry!" Mary said. "Sue, please! Make Rachel breathe again. Save her!" Mary had never felt so helpless in her life.

The siren got very loud now, and the crunch of gravel was unmistakable when the SUV pulled up. The siren cut off suddenly. She heard the car door slam. Further away, more sirens were sounding in the distance.

A single police officer ran through the pool gate, huffing slightly. Then he stopped and looked at Mary.

"Well, if it isn't Bloody Mary herself," the officer said, trying to make a joke. Mary had never felt so much hate and anger as she did at this moment. She pushed the Darkness back down. *Not now. Not now!*

"Sergeant Stadenko," Mary said. The Darkness was rising and falling. She had to keep it under control.

"Do you know CPR?" Sue gasped, out of breath. She clearly needed a break.

"Yeah, kind of," Stadenko said. He folded his arms across his chest. "But you seem to be doing just fine. I think I'd better keep my eye on Bloody Mary here."

"My name's Mary," Mary said icily. "Sir." This was going to be hard. *Don't think about throwing him into the pool and holding him down until the bubbles stop. Don't think. Don't think!* She focused on the slide at the far end of the pool. It trembled slightly. *Don't look at the cop!*

"You know, um, Mary... you've already established quite a record in our little community. First, you move in, and next thing you know, one of your little classmates? Dead. And now it looks like another classmate isn't going to make it."

The slide next to the cop began to shake harder. *Oh, please, don't hurt him,* she thought to herself. *It's only going to make things worse!*

"I thought you two were close, so I wasn't expecting this. We tend to keep an eye on outsiders who come in and corrupt our town."

Some of the bolts holding the pool ladder to the deck broke loose. Only Mary noticed. Sue was desperately trying to save her daughter's life. Stadenko was smiling like a shark zooming in for the kill. The other siren was loud now.

"I thought you were a little young to start killing, but I guess you already know how, huh, Bloody Mary?"

The second bolt holding the pool ladder down broke just as the siren cut off in front of the house. A man and a woman came running in with equipment bags. They quickly took over for Sue. The male paramedic began rescue breathing and chest compressions, while the female paramedic began looking for other injuries.

The woman let out a gasp. "We have what appears to be a skull fracture," she said quietly to her partner. She continued her survey of the young patient. Were those ligature marks or abrasions around the young teen's neck? She quickly pulled out her radio. "EMS-2, East Regional Dispatch," she said, trying to sound calm and in control.

"Go ahead, EMS-2," the dispatcher from before responded.

"Dispatch, send LE backup. At least get them started in this direction. This may be a possible Code One."

"Roger, EMS-2. Sending them now." The dispatcher knew that this address would be crawling with cops soon. No cop could resist a Code One. Homicides were too rare. They'd all want a piece of this.

"Sergeant," the female paramedic called Stadenko over. Once out of earshot, she said, "This is a crime scene." She went back to work. Stadenko smiled cruelly.

The ladder fell into the pool.

CHAPTER FOURTEEN

"You're not going to ask my daughter any more of your insinuating questions," Jimmy shouted at Stadenko in the kitchen of the big house.

"You mean your adopted daughter?" Stadenko sneered. "Yeah, we know all about you."

The house was now officially a crime scene. The county medical examiner had pronounced Rachel dead about an hour after the first responders arrived. They had worked valiantly on reviving her, but Rachel didn't come back.

The Darkness was stronger than ever, but Mary fought it back. She didn't even dare to imagine anything about Stadenko at all, as she was well aware of what could happen. She knew... if she thought about something, it would happen.

"Sergeant Stadenko?" said a CSI officer who had come into the kitchen. "Did you recover the young lady's phone?"

"No, I ain't got no phone," Stadenko snarled in the direction of no one in particular. "Kids these days are just coddled too much. Maybe it's in the pool."

"We looked, Sergeant," the officer said. "The only things that were in the pool that shouldn't have been there were the slide and, of course, the young lady. We should recover the phone. It may contain evidence as to what happened."

"Incompetents!" Stadenko spat out. "I bet it's down there, and you guys with your fancy degrees just can't look close enough!"

Stadenko got up and walked out the patio door. There was a big puddle on the patio. Mary saw it. Stadenko didn't. The Darkness won (briefly) and Stadenko lost his footing. He made a huge splash.

Mary let herself smile for a whole second.

"Somebody should get him out of the pool," Mary said. "He's contaminating the crime scene."

The crime tech hadn't moved. He did smile at Mary, though.

"Mary," the CSI tech said, "I'm going to take you downtown to the station for questioning. Special Agents Owens and Armstrong need to talk to you."

"About what?" Mary asked.

"Well, they are going to want to know about you and Rachel."

"Like what about us?"

"Probably everything starting from the first day you saw her till now."

Mary cut the tech short. "What about our friendship? Are they going to wonder about that? Rachel was my best friend."

"Look. There's nothing for you to be worried about as long as you tell the truth and, of course, you had nothing to do with the murder."

Mary lowered her head.

"Mary," Nacole whispered, coming in behind her, "we need to do what the man says. Let's just get this nightmare over with."

"Mom," Mary said with a quiver in her voice, "this nightmare will never be over for me now. I miss her." Tears rolled down her cheek. Nacole reached for her purse, pulled out a tissue, and wiped the tears from her daughter's face.

"I know, sweetie. I miss her too. Let's just get up and get this over with."

"Nacole," Jimmy said. "I think I'll stay here and guard this house. There will be tons of people around here. I don't want to leave the place unattended. They'll steal us blind."

"Sorry, Jimmy. You will need to go with us for questioning."

"That's OK, Jimmy. I can keep watch when you go," Stadenko smiled. "You don't have to worry about anything. Just take Bloody Mary with you."

Jimmy narrowed his eyes, stepping toward Stadenko. "You need to leave now, Stadenko, before I come over there and whoop your ass."

Jimmy looked at where that voice came from. It was the CSI tech. He looked like he had had enough. "And go dry yourself off before you destroy their floor." Stadenko turned and walked out the door.

"That crazy bastard," was all the CSI tech said.

CHAPTER FIFTEEN

Lt. Owen came into the conference room where Mary was sitting. As she came in, she closed the door and sat down across the table from her, pulled out her pocket recorder, and set it on the table slightly off-center, yet between the two of them. She immediately pushed the red record button so that no part of the upcoming conversation would be missed.

The detective looked at Mary and said, "I'm kind of forgetful at times, so I make sure to do everything so I don't miss anything. I mean, you might say something now that no one thinks is important, but it might lead us to the bad guy. I'm sure you understand, right? With that being said, you don't mind if I record all this, do you?"

Jimmy was sitting next to Mary and was listening very closely to every word the detective was saying.

"Yes, Detective, that would be fine," he said.

Nacole nodded her consent, and Mary followed. Jimmy had been watching his daughter, and as Mary nodded, he couldn't help but tell her, "Out loud, Mary. Use your words to tell Detective Owen that it's alright to record this."

Mary grew increasingly frustrated with the way her dad was taking the lead here. But regardless, she growled, "I agree."

"Do you have any questions for us before we get started, Mary?" Lt. Owen asked politely.

"Yeah, I have one... are you guys going to search my room?"

It was obvious based on the detective's face that this question surprised her. "Well... that's a good question. I can only say this. I won't be searching it. I can't answer for CSI. Your room is where you and Miss Moore first spotted Rachel in the pool correct?"

Mary's eyes darkened as she looked around the room. "Yes." She wished she could launch them all into outer space.

"Honey, I know this isn't easy. This is just part of the job. You want to help us with this, right? Detectives need to document everything because they don't know at first what might be important. I've seen it before, as I mentioned earlier, where little things that nobody at first noticed ended up cracking cases. You want justice for what happened here, right?"

Mary didn't answer. Instead, she looked at Jimmy, clearly lost and trying to take it all in. The detective noticed. "Would it make you feel better if we obtained a search warrant for the entire house?"

Without hesitation, Jimmy looked at the detective and said, "Yes, it would."

"So, Mary, tell me about Rachel." The lieutenant was prepared for Mary to take as long as she needed. The red light was on, the recorder was working.

Mary visibly relaxed as she began to talk about Rachel to the police. She explained how they met, the terrible pool party, how Rachel basically became Mary's protector at the new school.

As Mary continued to tell the detective details of Rachel, the officer eventually said, "Mary, excuse me for just a moment, but from the way you're telling the story, it sounds like she was more than just a protector. I take it you two were really close?"

"We were," Mary said succinctly.

The detective wanted more, so she responded to that with silence. It was more than Mary could take; she cried, and the tears began to run down her face. Mary had been holding up pretty well, but now she was breaking down entirely in sobs.

"Pausing recording," Lt. Owen said. She looked at her watch and made a note of the time. She went over and hugged the poor girl, who then bawled, letting out the pain. Jimmy and Nacole stood nearby, holding each other, while the other officer, Detective Armstrong, folded his hands in his lap and looked on.

After a while, Mary composed herself, blew her nose, and took a deep breath. "Lt. Owen, thank you. I think I can answer more questions now."

Owen nodded gently. "OK, Mary." They turned on the recorder. "Let's try this again. Take your time. So... tell me again what happened before you looked out the window and spotted

Rachel in the pool. You and Rachel rode home from school together. Did you two fight?"

"Fight? No."

"OK. Tell me everything you remember," Lt. Owen continued. "No matter how small it may seem, don't leave any detail out."

Mary told the story of how they both came home, how she saw Rachel go into her house to get her swimsuit. While waiting, Mary had gotten something to eat, turned on the stupid game show, and realized that a half-hour had passed since she got home and Rachel hadn't arrived yet.

"And you called her? From your landline or your mobile device?" Armstrong asked.

"My cellphone," Mary said. "I guess that's a mobile device."

"Do you have it with you?"

"Yeah." She pulled it out of her jeans pocket.

"May I take a look at it?" Armstrong asked. She handed the cop her phone without thinking, and he pulled up the call history. Mary had no idea that her phone kept track of the calls that she had made. Armstrong looked and saw calls to Rachel and one to Rachel's house. He closed the screen and put the phone on the table.

"I know this is going to be hard, Mary," Lt. Owen said, "but you're doing great. There might be some evidence on your phone. Can we keep it for a little while? Just to check it out?"

Mary looked horrified. To separate a schoolgirl from her phone was brutal, but Nacole said, "Let them have the phone, Mary. It's worth it if it helps them find who did this to Rachel."

"Armstrong, make a note to get a warrant for a forensic exam of the phone," Lt. Owen said. She knew it might be possible to trace the location of the phone within a few feet during the time Mary claimed to be alone. What was she doing? That tracking device called a mobile phone might tell, and for Mary's sake, the detective hoped she was telling the truth. Well, she was trained to follow the evidence. Her own mobile phone rang, and she paused the recording once again. She was surprised that she hadn't silenced it, then she realized she was getting a call from one of the few numbers that could get past the 'Silent' setting. One was the sheriff, the other was the medical examiner. It was the latter calling right now.

Owen stepped outside the conference room, talked briefly to the official, then stepped back in.

"Folks, that's going to wrap things up for tonight. The crime scene people have just arrived at your house, and you can expect them to be there most of the night." Lt. Owen looked in her purse and found a business card. "The department has a deal with the DoubleTree Hotel. We'll cover your hotel bills while we have to keep you out of the house. Is that OK?"

Jimmy and Nacole just nodded. They were both just numb now. What Lt. Owen did not tell them was that if Mary was charged and convicted, the DoubleTree bill would be rolled into the court costs they'd have to pay. No reason to stress them out anymore, she thought. *Maybe they won't have to worry,* but the detective had her doubts. A couple scenarios of what happened were already playing out in her head, and none of them were good.

"Anything else we should know right now before we get out of here?"

"Yeah." Mary said. "Whenever Rachel and I would lay out by the pool to sunbathe, our creepy neighbor was up in the window of his house watching. I wanted to call the cops, but I never was fast enough to actually see him. I just saw his curtains move."

"Hmm. Interesting." Was this lady slick enough to try a ruse like this? She didn't know. "Have a good evening, folks, or at least as good as you can under these circumstances. And please, take these Human House leftovers with you. You might get hungry later."

Armstrong and Owen knew perfectly well which room the family would occupy: the one they had wired with microphones and hidden cameras. None of it could be used in court, of course, but if Mary broke down and confessed to her parents, they'd be able to get her to confess to them, too. All they had to do was send an online command to start recording—ah, the Internet of Things was amazing!

CHAPTER SIXTEEN

County Medical Examiner Vladimir "Call me Wally" Schmitt, M.D., saw a lot of violent death, and it no longer bothered him. But seeing a violent death of a young girl still made him a little bit queasy. And this one was a homicide, no doubt.

"We'll have to send her to the capital for a full forensic... autopsy," he told Owen and Armstrong, "but I wanted you to have the preliminary findings as soon as possible."

The two detectives wore personal protective gear in the chilly atmosphere of the medical center morgue. Schmitt pulled the sheet off the young girl's body. The two cops immediately saw what the paramedics on the scene saw: a massive, bloody contusion on the back of the girl's head, and a broad ligature mark around her neck.

"As you can see, the blunt-force trauma to the back of her head is obvious," Schmitt said, pointing with the end of his pen. "I'd say the weapon looks like a big crowbar or a hefty piece of steel pipe. And look at these tiny abrasions on the bruise on her neck: that's consistent with being strangled with a leather belt, and there are a couple of cuts right here where the buckle dug into her skin."

Armstrong started thinking of his own little girl, who had just turned eleven, and he started to sweat. Yeah, Mary's father would have a crowbar as part of his construction work. Did he have a black leather belt? Another search warrant.

Schmitt then pointed his pen. "Obviously, we looked for signs of sexual assault, and unfortunately, we found them."

Armstrong and Owen both looked up sharply. This terrible case had gotten worse.

"You'll notice fresh abrasions here, here, and... here," the medical examiner said. "These are consistent with a very forceful assault. You'll also notice these bruises here and here and here elsewhere on her body. She was very much alive when this took place, and she fought back hard. I'd say she was overwhelmed by a much stronger attacker."

"So this wasn't done by a kid," Armstrong said.

"Very unlikely," Schmitt said. "I'd look for an adult male."

"You're sure it was a male?" Owen said. Schmitt smiled tightly.

"Um, you're getting ahead of me," the doctor said, "but women can't leave the kind of DNA evidence we found. We collected a rape kit along with the material under her nails. There was blood under her nails. Like I said, she fought hard."

Schmitt, Owens, and Armstrong stood in silence, looking at Rachel's bruised, battered body. It seemed so tiny, so fragile. Lt. Owens felt her knees go weak. "Oh, my god," she said, almost as a prayer.

"We'll run the DNA, and if the guy is a registered sex offender, his DNA is on file," Armstrong said. "Simple."

Schmitt shook his head. "Not so simple, Detective Armstrong," the doctor said. "It's very rare for sex offenders to re-offend, despite what you see on TV. In fact, the only category of offender less likely to re-offend is murderers, and that's because people convicted of murder go to prison and never get out. Sex offenders get out, and usually stay out of trouble."

"Uh, one more thing," Owen said. "Do you know if the hospital or the paramedics or anybody recovered the victim's cell phone?"

"I have the vic's personal effects, her clothing, waiting to turn them over to the crime lab for processing," Schmitt said, "but there's no cell phone in there."

"We need to find that cell phone," Owen said. "I wrote down the number from Mary's phone. Contact Central Dispatch and have them get with the wireless provider to ping the phone and get a geolocation. I know what we need to do now."

"What's that?" Armstrong asked.

"We need to go visit Wilson, the neighbor, and ask him a few questions. Right now, I think he is our lead suspect."

"What about Mary?" Armstrong asked.

"You remember what Schmitt said. There was no way a young girl would be strong enough to do that, plus the DNA evidence. It had to be an adult male that we're looking for. Let's go talk to Wilson first and see what he has to say."

CHAPTER SEVENTEEN

"Remember, this is still the shoeleather phase—talking to all the neighbors," Owen told her partner. "Once this Wilson character becomes a person of interest, officially, we'll bring him in and really talk to him."

"When will that happen?"

"When we have more than just the sense that he's a creep."

Armstrong pressed the doorbell, and in a few minutes, John Wilson came to the door. He was nearly six feet tall with slightly shaggy gray hair and a beard more neatly trimmed than his hair. He was wearing black jeans, a black turtleneck, and black work boots that didn't show much wear.

"Officers! How nice to see you!" he smiled, extending his hand to Owen. "One gold bar on your uniform… does that make you a lieutenant in your department, ma'am?"

"It does," Lt. Owen said. "I'm Detective Lt. Owen, and this is my partner, Detective Armstrong. I'm wearing my uniform in sympathy with him. He looks like someone you'd want to throw out of your house if he's in plainclothes."

Wilson eyed Armstrong's tattooed arms, beard, and hair.

"I can see that," Wilson said. "Would you please come in? Would you like some coffee? An aperitif?"

Armstrong wasn't even sure what that was. "No, sir, we're fine."

"I guess you're just doing your due diligence, talking to everyone who might know something about that horribly sad situation next door. I'm still processing it… poor Rachel. Drowned in the neighbor's pool. You know, when that family bought that house and put in the pool, I just had a terrible feeling something bad was going to happen there. Please, sit down."

Owen and Armstrong sat on Wilson's couch in a large living room with windows on two sides. On the third wall hung a large oil portrait of a young girl in a sundress, smiling broadly. The girl was about eight years old. With a shock, Armstrong recognized the girl.

"Is that Rachel Moore?" he blurted out.

"Yes," Wilson said, smiling. "Isn't she lovely?"

"Um, Mr. Wilson," Owen said, "isn't it a little weird to have a big portrait of the little girl across the street on your living room wall?"

"Oh, not at all," Wilson said smoothly. "I should explain. I'm a professional portrait painter. I'm very well known in the art trade, but I wouldn't expect a couple of small-town police officers to know that. That's not your fault. It's not the life you lead.

"But I travel all over the country painting people's portraits. My commissions generally run in the high six figures, and I pretty much work when I want to. Anyway, the Moores moved in across the road when Rachel was just a baby, and she was so adorable. I began sketching her. My studio is full of sketches and studies of her, but that oil is my first full portrait of her.

"She liked to play games with me, like hide-and-seek. She liked to hide in the attic, and I'd pretend I couldn't find her. She liked to work in my garden with me, planting flowers. She was my little buddy."

"Then I suppose her sudden death hit you hard," Armstrong said.

"I don't like to repeat myself, officer, but as I told you before, I'm still processing this tragedy," Wilson sighed. "I guess we all react differently to trauma."

"So what happened today, from your viewpoint? What were you doing? What did you see? What did you hear?" Armstrong asked.

Wilson sat up a little straighter in his armchair and looked a little offended. "I was sitting right here, reading *Architectural Digest* and salivating over a delightful home in an exquisite setting on Lake Michigan. I heard shouts from next door.

"Now, ever since that... family... moved in, the noise level has just increased by orders of magnitude, but this sounded almost hysterical. I ran up to my bedroom and looked out the window. There, in the pool, were Mary—that's the name of that dreadful girl next door—and Sue Moore and my little buddy Rachel. They all were wearing street clothes! How trashy! But then I realized that Rachel wasn't splashing. She wasn't even moving! I knew intuitively at that point that poor Rachel must have fallen into the pool, and I was watching a major tragedy unfold before my very eyes.

"Well, officers, I can't swim. I confess I've never set aside time to learn CPR. All I can do is paint pretty pictures. But I did do my duty as a good citizen, and I called 911 on my bedroom extension. There was nothing else I could do, and it was too terrifying to watch my little buddy's life slip away beneath my gaze. I simply closed the curtains, and I sat on my bed and wept.

"I heard the sirens of the police and the ambulance arriving, but I realized that I heard no sirens when the ambulance left." Wilson looked far off for a moment. "I know enough about the world to know that when someone has perished, hurrying will do them no good." He reached into his jeans pocket and pulled out a tissue, dabbing the corner of his eye. "It was manifest that Rachel had passed." He looked down at the carpet for a while. The officers silently traded glances.

"I guess that's all I can tell you," Wilson finally said. "Are you sure you wouldn't like a drink? Investigating a child's tragic drowning death has to be a strain."

Owen ignored that. "This is a lot more than you told that TV station at six o'clock," she said.

Wilson snorted. "That ditzy microphone-holder didn't ask," he said.

"So you're an artist and Rachel posed for you, Mr. Wilson," Owen said. "What kind of poses?"

"Oh, all kinds," Wilson said. "She took such delight in letting me sketch her or photograph her. I have a cabinet full of studies from the time she was a toddler until this past spring. I gave some of the best to her mother, and she was gasping with rapture every time I'd give her a new one."

"Would you mind if we looked in your files?" Armstrong asked.

"I would," Wilson said. "I fail to see what my professional product and work methods have to do with the tragic drowning death of a girl, or are you just fishing? I assure you, I'm not going to bite!"

"And we had to ask," Owen said. "Our professional work methods require that." She smiled sweetly.

"So, do you live here by yourself, Mr. Wilson?" Armstrong finally asked.

"Well, I don't know what that has to do with anything, but yes, I do," Wilson said. "I'm a confirmed bachelor. I fell in love with a girl once, but, sadly, she died much too young. Now, my work—my art—is my love."

"So why this police interest in my personal life?" Wilson said. "It seems obvious what happened: Someone left the gate unlocked, my little buddy went in, slipped, and fell into the pool. By the time they found her, it was too late." He dabbed his eye again with the tissue.

"Your bedroom overlooks the patio and the pool," Armstrong said. "You ever watch the girls sunbathe?"

"Officer, are you paid to be rude? Of course not!"

"Mary, the, uh, dreadful girl next door, as you put it, told us she thought you were watching them," Owen said. "She said she saw the curtains in your window move a lot."

"Well, of course she did," Wilson said. "That little snitch. This is an old house, and it's not air-conditioned. I keep a fan running all the time, so of course the curtains move."

"May we see?"

"No. I've had enough of your police-state nosiness about things that have nothing to do with the tragic death of this little girl," Wilson huffed. "Are we finished? Yes. This confabulation is finished. Lieutenant, Detective, I'll show you the door. Have a good evening!"

A citizen has a perfect right to ask police officers to leave if the officers don't have at least probable cause to stay. The investigators left and went to their waiting squad car.

As they sat down, Armstrong broke the silence. "Con-fabu-what-the?" he grinned.

"Confabulation," Owen said, stifling a giggle. "I think it's a nine-dollar word for conversation."

"We got anything on artist boy here?" Armstrong asked.

"Not that we can use right now," Owen said. "But we'll have to ask Sue Moore about it."

As they watched, Wilson's garage door opened. He was at the wheel of a brand-new-looking Ford pickup. The garage door closed as he hit Powderkeg Road and roared off into the night.

"Should we follow him?" Owen asked.

"Not in a marked unit," Armstrong said. "He seems like the type to claim harassment."

"Nice truck."

"Yeah, but every third peckerwood in the county has one like it, if not so new." Armstrong turned his attention to the police car's computer screen and noted a text message: *R MOORE PHONE RESPONDED TO PING.*

The message gave a location in latitude and longitude down to eight decimal places. "Well, let's see where it is," he said, copying the coordinates and pasting them into Google Maps. In a couple of seconds, a map of Powderkeg Road popped up on the squad car's screen.

"Gotcha!" Armstrong said. "That's Mary's house."

Owen looked at the screen. "Um, no it's not," she said. "That's Wilson's place."

Armstrong swore. "You're right." He zoomed in tighter on the screen, then switched the image from a map to a satellite image. "Yeah, that's his house all right," he said. "Looks like it might be in his bedroom. Warrant time!"

He minimized the Google map, called up the affidavit form for a search warrant, and quickly filled it out. "Um, what's the address?" he mumbled, spinning the car's spotlight onto Wilson's house until he found the house number. Armstrong quickly typed that in and sent the warrant request off to the magistrate judge on duty.

"Nice having a magistrate on call 24/7 for instant search warrants," Owen said. "I hear they do it all on iPads."

"Should we ask for help from the crime scene kids?"

"Yes," Armstrong said. "This is our scene, but if we accidentally screw it up, we'd never hear the end of it. Let's let them screw it up."

The computer chimed as a brand-new search warrant popped in. The car's printer was out of service, so Armstrong picked up a tablet, connected with Bluetooth to the car's computer, and walked the warrant onto his tablet.

"Let's get the kids and go find that phone."

Owen walked toward Wilson's house, waving her arms in the air and signaling the rest of the donut-eating crew to get off their asses and get ready to enter.

"Now, before we go in," Owen said, "me, Armstrong, and Stadenko." Armstrong lowered his head, doing everything he could not to laugh.

"Stadenko! Please wipe the donut glaze off your mouth and find one of your donut-eating buddies to go with you. Alright, now listen up! The four of us will go in, and I want the rest of you to form a perimeter around the house. I want all the exits—doors, windows, and any other possible way in or out of the house— guarded. No one gets in or out of this place while I'm in charge of this operation. I don't think he's here, but we can't take any chances on this one. Okay… everyone got it? Does everyone know what to do? Any questions? Alright, everyone, let's move and make me proud!"

As Owen reached the door and received the signal that everyone was in place, she knocked on the door. After the knock, she announced, "Open up… this is the police… search warrant!" Then, to be sure she made it official, she announced it again, "Open up! This is the police! Search warrant!" As she made the second announcement, the house remained silent and still.

Owen grabbed hold of the doorknob of the front door and announced over her whisper mic, "Entering, let's move in, everyone," so that everyone knew what was going on and that all movements would be coordinated. There wasn't room to screw this one up. She also wanted to make sure that the time of entry was recorded on the police tapes that would record each and every word uttered by the squad members.

Owen took her free hand and placed it upon her Glock, which was securely fastened in its holster, and pulled it out to a ready position while still keeping her other hand on the doorknob. As she pushed the door open, it swung silently with an eerie quality to it. And just like the eerie silence of the door, Owen found the house in the same state… silent. The breach was complete, and now it was time to execute the fine details of the warrant to get to the bottom of this saga.

Despite the house being quiet, Owen and her team couldn't afford to make any mistakes. There was no room for errors considering the high stakes of the case. Any slip could cost them the case, and Owen knew this. The house appeared to be empty;

however, Owen knew that looks could be deceiving, and until the house was cleared, she could not assume that there was no one inside. She had to move quickly but thoroughly, and she also had to ensure that her team did the same... no mistakes.

Owen, just above a whisper, which was enough for her mic to pick up, announced, "Everyone... be careful! My spidey senses are tingling, and I've got a bad feeling about this." Owen couldn't quite put her finger on it and explain her uneasiness; however, she just had an uneasy feeling about the whole thing.

The search team moved stealthily into the house and out of the doorway's "fatal funnel" of fire. As they moved, they ceaselessly scanned their surroundings. Foyer area... check... cleared, and next into the living room they went. The team's heads turned to the left, then to the right, then up to the overhead. Their moves seemed almost orchestrated, but they had to be on point and make sure that they didn't get sloppy.

Again, Owen broke radio silence in order to coordinate the teams that were depending on her expertise in this sort of thing.

"All right... listen up, Stadenko, you and your donut-eating buddies head upstairs and do a detailed sweep. And Stadenko, be careful of those stairs! Remember to watch your overhead, and as soon as you can, peek at your six to ensure no one takes a round in the back of the head. Got it? Armstrong and our team are going to sweep the rest of the first floor of the house so we can make sure it's clear. After we know it's clear, then we can start the actual search, but not a moment sooner. I don't want any surprises, and I want you all to walk out of here, especially so that Stadenko and his knuckleheads can live to eat another donut. Stay vigilant, gentlemen!"

Stadenko followed Owen's instructions and stealthily climbed the stairs with his team, while Owen and Armstrong remained downstairs. Both teams moved with precision, ensuring they didn't miss any nooks or crannies that could get anyone hurt during phase two. Despite their precision, this wasn't an everyday task for any of the team members, and so white knuckles were evident as they kept overly tight grips on the handles of their Glocks.

"Bottom team to top team… how are you doing?" soon came across the radios. No sooner than the question was asked, Stadenko announced, "Top team to bottom team, we're all clear up here. Top floor secure."

Owen gave a mental fist bump and replied, "Outstanding, top team! Well done! We're all secure down here as well. Bottom floor all clear."

Owen called the two teams together downstairs and gave the next set of instructions. "Alright everyone… nice job! We're moving into phase two, Operation No Stone Unturned. I want every—and I mean *every*—room searched with a fine-tooth comb! You miss something, and it will be your job! Do I make myself clear? There's something here, and it's our job to find it! No mistakes, gentlemen. A mistake will jeopardize the entire case, and I won't let that happen on my watch. Any questions?"

All the team members were silent as Owen barked out their marching orders, and then Owen gave the final command, "Now get to it!"

Shortly after the search began, Lt. Armstrong said, "Owen, come here. This looks like it could be John's bedroom."

John's room was a cluttered mess, with his worn clothes of who knows how many days strewn all over the room. A pair of tighty-whities with a brown racing stripe down the center of the crotch lay beside an old pair of faded blue jeans.

Then Lt. Armstrong broke the momentum of the search with a startling discovery. "Hey Owen, who's the little girl in all these pictures? They are everywhere. Isn't that Rachel?"

Owen quickly went to Armstrong's side and looked at the pictures that Armstrong had discovered stealthily.

After looking at the pictures, Owen confirmed Armstrong's suspicions by saying, "It sure looks like it, Armstrong." Owen took the pictures from Armstrong's grasp and inspected them more closely.

Owen squinted and pulled the pictures closer to her eyes, and the reality became more evident.

With this discovery, Owen announced, "Start looking through all of the drawers and underneath everything. That phone has to be here, and I want it found! Again, leave no stone unturned... not one!"

Owen was growing more angry, and the flames were now being fueled by the pictures of Rachel scattered throughout the room. Owen knew they had to find Rachel's phone, as it would be a critical part of their investigation.

After Owen and Armstrong had torn apart every square inch of John's room, Owen angrily exclaimed, "Damn it! Where is that damn phone?" Then, seemingly out of desperation, Owen looked across the room and shouted, "Stadenko! Did you find anything?"

Stadenko was almost afraid to respond but needed to be honest, "Nope... not a damn thing."

Owen couldn't settle for a loss, as the stakes were simply too high on this one. Owen slipped into an almost comatose state of concentration and then said, "It's got to be in this house somewhere. This is the most likely place." Then Owen looked at

Stadenko and asked, "Didn't they ping that phone, and didn't it show to be in this location?"

Stadenko, listening intently to Owen, said, "Yeah, they sure did. I'm sure it's here somewhere, but where is the big question."

Then Owen's eyes lit up with new life as she said, "Alright, Stadenko, here's what I want you to do. Get on your cell phone and call the department and have them call Rachel's phone. Tell them to not stop dialing the phone until they hear something from us. I don't know if it will work or not, but it's worth a try. Maybe we'll get lucky and hear it ring as long as the battery isn't dead."

Stadenko didn't hesitate a single moment. He reached into his front shirt pocket, pulled out his cell phone, and dialed up the department with a new sense of hope that this would work and would lead them right to the phone, which had now become a proverbial needle in a haystack.

"Yes," the male tech said. "We're looking for a particular cell phone."

"Give me the number," one of the other techs said. When she got it, she called it, and the investigators heard a phone go off above their heads. After a half-dozen rings, the call went to voicemail, and she ended the call.

"Let's find a stairway," she said. The group spied stairs at the back of the living room and raced up. Another call—and the ringing phone was still above them.

"What the… it's got to be in the attic!"

They searched around, looking for an entrance to the attic. In a back bedroom, they found a trap door and pulled it down. Quietly, both deputies pulled their sidearms and went first into the dark, dusty attic.

"It's clear," they announced. "And there are footprints in the dust up here."

"Don't move unless you have to," a female tech said. She called Rachel's phone again, and it sounded at the other end of the attic. "I'll go and retrieve it," she said. She climbed up to the hot, stifling attic, called the phone again to make it chime, and spotted it under an old chest of drawers. She found it and dropped it into an evidence bag just as the battery on the phone gave out.

"Guys, we're going to need another warrant for this whole house, and a warrant to search the phone," the male tech said.

The county magistrate quickly complied, and in minutes, John's house was surrounded by yellow crime scene tape. Just about then, a television van showed up on the road out front. The reporter and producer didn't really know anything, but it didn't stop them from going live and talking about it.

The phone was quickly taken to the sheriff's office, plugged into a charger, and brought back to life. A deputy, who had just received training in mobile-device forensics, put on blue nitrile gloves and began paging through the device. She quickly spotted an audio file, date-stamped that morning. She opened it, and it began to play.

"What you got in your hand?" a male voice said.

"That's my bathing suit, John," a girl's voice said. "I'm going over to Mary's house to go swimming."

The deputy shook her head. This was a smart girl—she started recording an audio note when she must have felt threatened. The deputy put her own phone next to Rachel's phone and began to record the sound coming from the girl's mobile device.

"It seems you've been going over there a lot lately," John said.

"She's my best friend."

"I thought I was your best friend," John said. "But I haven't seen you since Mary moved in. I thought you loved me, Rachel."

"I'm sorry, John," Rachel said. "I was going to tell you that I'm not going to go into your house anymore."

"Why not?" John asked. "Didn't you always have fun… when you came to visit?"

"I just don't want to," Rachel said. "It's not right."

There was a long pause.

"I knew this was going to happen when that family moved in with that… girl!" John's voice was louder now, closer to the phone that was picking up his voice, and she was talking louder, too.

"Calm down, John," Rachel said. "I gotta go. Mary's waiting."

"Don't leave!" John said. "I'm afraid I'll never see you again."

"John, it's better if we don't see each other again for a while."

Another long pause. "Listen, Rachel, I have a bunch of art supplies… I want you to have. I know how much you like to draw. They're up in the attic. I've been meaning to give them to you for a while now."

"I don't want your art supplies."

"Listen, I'm going to give you those art supplies, Rachel!"

"Fine. Go get them."

"I'll need your help to get them out of the attic, Rachel."

"Fine."

The recording thumped and rustled for a while. Apparently, the mobile device was in her school uniform skirt pocket. The deputy heard a loud squeak, as if from a rusty hinge, and a thump.

"Up the stairs, Rachel," John said. "You're going to help me find the art supplies. They're in a box."

More rustling and footsteps, and the trap-door ladder creaking. Rachel, beginning to think this was a bad idea and being all alone with John up in his attic, decided she needed to leave.

"I'm leaving, John."

"You're not going anywhere, Rachel."

"John! No! Stop! Put down the pipe, John! Don't hurt me! Look, I'll stop seeing Mary. I'll do anything you want me to do, John… John!"

The deputy gasped when she heard the metallic "clunk" followed by a skittering across the attic floor.

John's voice was far off now. "If I can't have you, Rachel, nobody is going to have you."

More thumps and scratching. A sickening feeling entered the room. The silence was worse than the rustling. The deputy began to cry, silently.

"Well, Rachel, you can't stay here," John's voice suddenly broke the silence.

The deputy heard thumps and the sound of Rachel's body sliding across the dusty floor, and a thumping down the stairs.

The trap door creaked shut, and the sound on the recording went dead silent. The deputy stopped the playback and broke down in sobs.

CHAPTER EIGHTEEN

Sheriff Jackson lumbered up to the podium once again. "Quiet, please!" Jackson shouted as he cleared his throat. He looked very official in his County Mounty hat. The sun was not nearly as bright as the last time they announced Eric's death, but habit was habit.

"We have another tragic event. A little girl whose name was Rachel Moore has been murdered. She's the second murder of our schoolchildren that we've had in two weeks. We have a suspect whose name is John Wilson. Anyone with knowledge of his whereabouts, please contact the Sheriff's Department by dialing 911. I have all of my available staff, plus a group of investigators, working on all that they can to find the suspect. For those curious, the Feds *are* involved, but of course, my department is leading the investigation. Questions?"

The local news people were having a field day, all of them grouped together like a gaggle of geese. It wasn't long before they had pulled Wilson's picture off Facebook, along with a picture of Rachel, also from Wilson's page.

Mary was sitting at home watching television when the special news bulletin came across the local television station.

"RACHEL MOORE, FOURTEEN-YEAR-OLD GIRL... MURDERED."

Mary listened intently and learned that the suspect in the case was a man by the name of John Wilson.

"MOM!" Mary shrieked, "COME HERE QUICK!"

Nacole, who was in the kitchen pouring a cup of coffee, came running into the living room.

"What's wrong, baby?" Nacole asked.

"It's Rachel!" Mary sobbed. "Mom, they showed a picture of her on the news!"

"I'm sorry, baby," Nacole said, sitting down beside her daughter. Nacole quietly set her coffee cup down on the table and pulled Mary tightly to her chest.

"Mom… I miss her terribly."

To which her mom replied as only a mother could, "I know, sweetie, I know."

"Mom, is this horrible nightmare ever going to end?"

"Yes, honey, it is. After they arrest John and throw his ass in prison, then things will start getting easier, I promise."

"I hope they kill him! And if they don't, I WILL!"

"Honey, they will take care of it. We need to leave it to the authorities."

"Throwing him in prison is not enough for what he did to her! He took away my best friend in the whole wide world!"

"I know, baby, I know. Remember that time heals all wounds."

"Mom, I will never forget her. NEVER."

"Baby, you don't have to," Nacole said. "She will always be with us in our thoughts. However, you will move on, I promise."

"Mom, are you… are you happy that I'm here?" Mary looked down at the floor.

"Happy! What do you mean?" Nacole didn't like this or where it might be going.

"I mean, I wasn't planned. I was an 'oops' baby. That's what Stadenko told me."

"Oh, honey," Nacole smiled. "I love you more than anything in the whole world. You should know that by now."

Mary looked up at her mom. "I know you lied to me. I know that."

"Yes, I did, and I'm sorry," Nacole said. "But I did it to protect you, and I'm not sorry about ever doing that."

"Protect me from what, Mom?" Mary's eyes narrowed. "If you would have been honest with me from the start, this whole thing would have been a whole lot easier!"

"I know," Nacole exclaimed. "I'm really sorry. But I was scared."

"I would have found out sooner or later, you know."

"Mary, I thought that all the stuff that you had told me was a bunch of BS! I mean, who would have believed that any of this stuff would have been possible?"

"Well…" Mary said after thinking for a second, "after everything that you, Dad… I mean, Jimmy… um… after what we all saw at the beach, you should have believed it."

"Honey, Jimmy and I were in shock. The psychologist told Jimmy and me that we were both crazy. They locked us up for months. They gave us all sorts of mind-altering drugs. By the time we got out, we didn't know if it all was real or not."

"Tell me about my real dad!" Mary demanded. Mary lay down and put her head on Nacole's lap. Nacole brushed Mary's hair with her fingertips.

"Calm down, honey. What do you want to know?"

"Everything," Mary smiled, snuggling up to her a little tighter.

"Well, he was amazingly good-looking, reddish-blond hair, about the same color as yours. He was the captain of the varsity football team. I fell in love with him the first time I saw him. Oh, gosh! That smile. It would make me melt like butter every time I looked at him, and I caught him looking back at me. His gorgeous blue eyes…

"I remember him taking me out to this little restaurant. I think it was called Mama Jane's Restaurant. He showed up at my door in this green piece of crap car he always drove. The music was always cranked up as loud as it could go. You could hear him from miles away. A few months before we graduated, his mom and dad bought him a new black Camaro for his graduation present. He didn't get to drive it much, though." Nacole slumped her head in tears.

Mary reached up, wiping away the tears that were flooding down her mother's face. "I'm sorry, sweetie, I didn't mean to cry."

Nacole sniffed and flipped her head back, shocked at the amount of tears. "Oh, God... I haven't cried like that in a while. I really must have needed it."

Nacole looked down at her daughter. Mary was almost a mirror copy of her mother, tears running down and all. "Are you okay?" she asked, her own tears forgotten.

"I'm fine..." Mary sobbed while using a sleeve to wipe up her own pain. "I just wish I could have met him; that's all."

"Me too, baby... me too."

The FBI had found Wilson's pickup truck in long-term parking at the local airport. Wilson, however, was nowhere to be found. Owen was sifting through the pickup, trying to find a tiny piece of evidence so she could continue with her search. Armstrong asked while tearing the back seat of the truck apart:

"So… have we found anything yet?"

Owen laughed sarcastically. "Are you kidding me? There's nothing here but a few newly burnt cigarette butts. We need to go inside and talk to one of the staff. One of them might remember him."

Owen and Armstrong walked inside and over to the ticket stand.

"Hello, ma'am," Owen said. "We're looking for this man. He goes by the name of John Wilson. Have you by chance seen him?" Armstrong pulled out a picture and showed it to the young lady.

"Is that the guy who killed that little girl they found in the neighborhood pool?"

"And how do you know so much?" Owen asked suspiciously.

"Umm… this has been plastered all over the news?"

Owen was silent for a moment. "Damn the news!" she shouted with a clear sense of frustration. "Will you check in the computer system and see if he might have bought a plane ticket?"

"Hold on just one moment, please," the lady said politely enough. "I'll punch his name into the computer, and it should only take a moment." Then her reply came, "I'm sorry, I was unable to find his name in our system."

"Damn, again!" Owen thought for a second. "How about any type of surveillance tapes, ma'am?"

"Do you have any idea how many cameras there are in this place? Hundreds! It would take months for someone to go through that many tapes. I'd have to get permission from someone above my pay grade. I don't want to get into trouble…"

"Well, look," Armstrong started. "How many entrances are there at this airport?"

"About nine," the lady responded.

"Well, how about you just give us the surveillance footage you have that monitors the entrances?"

"OK… but sir," the lady said, "that's going to take some time."

"How much time?" Owen asked.

"A couple of hours, at least," she replied.

"We will wait," Owen said.

Owen and Armstrong waited and then took all the surveillance footage back to their office to be reviewed. After a couple of hours of long days of watching boring tape, they discovered nothing new. The question that remained? Would they ever find Wilson?

Rachel's funeral would assuredly bring out the entire town, so the decision was made to hold it at First Presbyterian Church, the largest church in town.

"MOM!" Mary shouted. "Where are you? I need your help!"

Mary flopped down on the floor and covered her face to cover up her tears.

"What's wrong, sweetie?" Nacole asked.

"I can't do this; I can't stand to see her like that."

"Well, do you just want to stay here? People will understand if you do."

"Mom, I don't give a damn about the people! I hate them all! I hate it here! I want to leave, to move far away!"

"We can't, Mary, you know that. We spent every dollar we had buying and remodeling our house. This will be the hardest day, but then we all can begin to heal. You have to trust me."

"Mom, if I go, I don't want anyone to know I'm there. I don't want to be humiliated in front of everyone."

Nacole hesitated. "I will talk to Lt. Owen. Maybe she can make that happen." Nacole grabbed her cell phone out of her pocket and dialed Owen's cell phone number.

"Hello, Nacole, what's up? Is everything OK?"

"It's fine," Nacole answered. "I guess... uh... maybe... I mean, Mary wants to go to the wake. Except she doesn't want to be seen by anyone because she doesn't want any drama."

"We can make that happen," Owen said. "So, what time do you want us to be there?"

"Around seven should be fine."

A few hours later, they found themselves at the wake. As Mary made her way, Armstrong kept an eye on the crowd. Mary and her parents pulled in at the back of the parking lot. Jimmy and Nacole stepped out first. Jimmy opened up the back door of the SUV.

"Wow, Mary," Owen said. "You look so beautiful." Mary was wearing a red dress, Rachel's favorite color.

"I don't feel beautiful," Mary answered. "To be honest with you, I feel stupid. As stupid as you must be with your lack of progress on my best friend's murder."

"MARY, apologize to Lt. Owen. That was very rude."

"I'm not apologizing to anyone."

"I'm sorry," Nacole said. "She's just having a bad day, obviously. All of us are."

Mary and her family were escorted by Owen through the back door of the church and upstairs to the balcony. The church's massive pipe organ was in the choir loft, and Owen passed out earplugs.

"Are you kidding me?" Mary growled. "This is stupid!"

"You were the one who wanted to hide," Nacole said. "Now live with it, or we will leave." Mary looked up at Nacole with narrowed eyes. Nacole looked coldly back. She understood that her daughter was upset, but she was still her mother.

"I would burn this whole place down if I could only throw fireballs like my Aunt Grace!" Mary said under her breath.

The service began, and after a few minutes, Mary could no longer stand all the crying. The fact that her best friend was lying downstairs all alone in that massive room upset her. All she could think about was never seeing Rachel again and wanting everyone else dead. Mary fell to the floor and raised her head. Her eyes darkened, her fingernails dug into the wooden floorboards.

The massive church began to shake. The pipe organ let out its last puff of air. Everyone began to run out of the church, screaming and covering their heads from the falling debris. Mary stared at Rachel's casket as the podium started to shake violently enough to cause the casket lid to close, locking it forever.

"No one deserves to see her again," Mary said to herself.

Nacole lowered her head and saw Mary's darkened eyes.

"Stop it, Mary!" Nacole shouted. "Stop! Before someone dies!"

Mary's body was shaking from the build-up of stress, emotion, and anxiety. Nacole bent over and shook Mary's numb body.

"Wake up!" Nacole shouted, slapping Mary across her face. Mary's eyes returned to normal, and she collapsed back to the floor.

Jimmy pushed through the crowd, squatted down, and picked up his daughter's limp, lifeless body. He ran down the stairs and out the door, with Nacole and Owen running right behind.

"Take her to the car!" Owen ordered.

Armstrong was doing all he could to control the crowd. Jimmy laid Mary down on the grass beside their SUV.

"Is she OK?" Owen asked.

Mary opened her eyes, now wet and clear. She hesitated and shook her long blonde hair in the wind. "What happened?" Mary asked.

"Thank God, sweetie, you're okay! You scared me half to death!" Jimmy yelled emphatically.

"I'm fine... or at least I think I am. What happened in there?" Mary asked, completely bewildered. "I don't remember anything at all. All I remember is falling to the floor; after that, everything went blank," she explained.

"I think there was an earthquake," Owen declared.

"Is everyone OK?" Mary asked.

Owen responded first. "I don't know for sure, but I think so. We'll just have to wait until Armstrong gets back. He's trying to control the situation as far as I could tell."

"What do you think happened, Mary?" Nacole asked sarcastically with a tight smile. Mary looked at her mother and seethed, seeing the sarcasm in her mother's tone.

"I don't know, Mom," Mary said again in a hateful tone. "I passed out."

Nacole turned and walked a few feet away, covering her mouth as she tried not to scream.

"We need to get Mary home. It's been a rough day for all of us," Jimmy said to the officer.

"I agree," Owen answered. Jimmy reached out his hand to Mary, who was still sitting on the ground, and pulled his daughter to her feet.

"Come on, Mom!" Mary shouted. Nacole had turned and was making her way back to the SUV at this point.

"Are you OK, Mom?" Mary asked, using the same sarcastic tone her mother had used on her. She gave her mother a little grin.

"I'm fine. Just get your little ass in the car," Nacole said curtly.

Owen turned, wondering what she had missed. Why were they suddenly fighting? Strange.

Nacole wondered to herself if Owen would ever figure it out.

CHAPTER NINETEEN

The next day, Wilson had not been found. Mary's school was still out pending the investigation of the murders of Erick and Rachel. But Mary's school trip to the state capitol building was still on. The school's staff thought it would be a good idea to do all they could to get the kids' minds off the murders that had rocked the community.

"Mary, are you out of bed yet? You have to get ready; you know I volunteered to be one of the chaperones, so I can't be late!" Nacole exclaimed while throwing on her jacket. "And where are my damn car keys!" she yelled with a panicked voice.

"Mom, come here," Mary said in a nasally voice.

"What is it? OMG, you're not even out of bed yet."

"I'm not going."

"Why not?"

"Because it will suck! I'll have to listen to the whispering sounds of 'Bloody Mary' the whole trip. Plus, Rachel still isn't in the ground after that earthquake. It just doesn't feel right going without her being buried."

"Well, what do you want to do all day, stay here by yourself?" Nacole asked.

"I will probably go swimming."

"Oh, hell no, you're not! They still haven't found that pervert Wilson, and he could be anywhere." She gave in a little and then added, "Alright, fine. I'll call your dad, and I'll have him call you every few minutes or so to make sure you're okay."

Mary mumbled in response, "No, Mom, I just need this day to be by myself to think and maybe get my head straight. And if you call Dad, he will be calling me every few minutes. I just want to be left alone. Maybe I'll just lay here and sleep all day."

"Well, you have to promise me that you'll stay inside and lock the doors. Then I'll be somewhat okay with your decision. However, you have to promise that you'll do what I ask and absolutely not go swimming."

"Okay, fine, Mom, I promise." Mary replied with swollen eyes. She was flopping back and forth on her bed while covering her face with one of her pillows.

"I'll see you after a while then, okay?"

"Okay, Mom. Bye."

Nacole pulled her bedroom door closed and ran down the spiral staircase.

"Now, where did my damn keys go again?" Nacole's eyes darkened as her keys came flying off the top of the refrigerator and slammed into her hands, almost hard enough to hurt.

Mary heard the living room door slam closed and the sound of her mom pulling out of the driveway and leaving her in solitude.

"Okay, I have to hurry now!" Mary thought.

Mary leaped from her bed, tossed off her nightgown, and ran to her closet, where she pulled out her school uniform. She slid on the short pleated skirt and then her blouse. She tucked her blouse neatly down inside the pleated skirt and knelt down to put on her black school shoes.

"Now where is my school jacket?" Mary inquired of the quietness that surrounded her while she danced around the room. As she located it, she exclaimed with a sense of relief, "There it is!"

Mary ran down the stairs, and as she reached the bottom, she realized that she had forgotten her cell phone. "Shoot, my damn cell phone," she said in just above a whisper.

Mary turned and ran back up the stairs into her room, quickly found her phone, turned back around with great urgency, and again returned down the stairs she had just run up.

Mary was exhausted by this point. She felt her pockets with the palm of her hand and exclaimed, "Alright, that should be everything I need."

Mary ran outside, slamming the back door behind her while doing her best to avoid being seen by any of her nosy neighbors. It was still very early in the morning, about seven o'clock. She hopped on her bike from a full run and pedaled as fast as she could down the road to her next destination.

Mary stopped at a one-way bridge that extended over the lake.

"This is perfect," she thought. Mary stepped off her bike and walked it to the water's edge. When she reached the edge of the lake, she tossed the bike into the cool water. As the bike hit the surface, making a significant splash, it was totally submerged in only seconds.

"Wow!" Mary mumbled to herself while looking for a hiding spot. "That tree beside the road will be perfect."

Mary stepped across the ditch line, which was hidden behind a giant oak tree.

"This is perfect! All I have to do is wait." Mary sat down on the muddy ground, twiddling her fingers and biting her fingernails. As she sat on the ground, she could hear the sound of a motorized vehicle coming her way. Along with the sound of the motor, she could hear the sounds of music playing and kids singing.

"It has to be them," Mary thought to herself.

Mary peeked out from behind the big oak tree as she watched the yellow school bus rolling her way.

"Wait!" Mary thought, and then once again, "Wait, WAIT!"

Mary stepped out from behind the tree and into the middle of the two-lane country road. As she did, she looked down while smiling.

"These double yellow lines should be about center," Mary surmised as the bus drew closer and had almost reached her.

It was obvious that the bus driver was distracted by what the kids on the bus were doing. He was so distracted that he didn't see Mary, in her school uniform, standing perfectly in the middle of the road. As the bus drew even closer, Mary raised her head, and her eyes darkened as she made eye contact with the driver.

"Oh my god! Mary!" the driver shouted. As he did, he stomped the brakes, and there was no response from the bus's braking system. As the brakes failed to activate, the driver took evasive action and swerved to miss Mary. As he did, the students and the faculty on the bus were thrown about like rag dolls being tossed across a playroom.

Meanwhile, Nacole was on the bus, gazing out the windshield at her daughter, who was still standing in the road, unfazed by the chaos. Mary rapidly swung her head to the left, and the bus followed in suit like a string puppet. Eventually, the bus slammed against a hillside, which launched the bus into the air and into the lake.

Mary ran quickly to the edge of the bank as the bus was still afloat. As she stood there, she could hear the distinct sounds of the kids on the soon-to-be-sinking bus screaming, crying, and begging for help as they tried feverishly to climb out the windows and doors of the bus.

Mary's eyes had darkened once again, and she willed the bus's front door and the emergency exit door to lock down tight. Mary then nodded toward the bus, and as she did, the windows all started to slam shut. Everyone on the bus could see Mary standing on the hill, and as she stood there, the bus's occupants screamed mercilessly for help. Mary continued to watch as the occupants helplessly tried to pry their way out of the bus. However, after some time, the bus slowly began to sink. As the bus took its seemingly last breath and became fully submerged, there was an eerie silence... no more sound... just silence.

Mary's eyes widened as she stood on the bank. As she overlooked the lake, the chaos of desperation had now subsided, and a calm and peace fell over the lake. The sun's rays reflected off the crisp, cool water, casting an almost irresistible blue hue over the lake. There were no more waves at this point—just calm and peace.

Mary started to make her way down the steep embankment, the mud slipping as her fingers dug deeply into the ground. As Mary reached the bottom of the embankment, she carefully made her way to the water's edge. She squatted down, reached her hands, now clasped together, into the water. As she scooped up the water in her hands and let it fall over her head and body, she then stuck her fingers into the mud, digging them deep into its essence. Mary smeared the mud onto her face like war paint.

Mary then lifted her head and rapidly looked across the lake, trying to discern what the noise in the distance was. The noise sounded like water splashing, though she wasn't quite sure. Mary turned her head left to right, then stood up and surveyed the rest of the lake. Mary squinted her eyes and raised her hand to her brow in an attempt to reduce some of the glare reflecting off the water's surface.

Mary watched as the water rippled, and then a blond head popped to the top of the water.

"HELP!" they screamed.

Mary backed up tight against the muddy bank.

"Oh my god, not everyone's dead!" Mary cried quietly under her breath.

Mary turned and pawed her way up the muddy embankment. Regardless of her best efforts, she found herself sliding right back down the embankment to the bottom. As Mary reached the bottom once again, she could hear the person screaming once again.

"Mom, is that YOU?" Mary shouted back.

"Help, please help me!" Nacole screamed.

Mary collapsed to her knees, panic unmistakable in her eyes. Mary covered her face and broke out into tears. As she stood in place, allowing her emotions to stream down her face, she once again heard helpless screaming coming from Nacole.

Then unexpectedly, Mary heard Nacole excitedly exclaim, "Something keeps grabbing my leg!" and with that, she was gone.

Mary stood up with a straight posture, and by this time, her tears had subsided. Mary scanned the top of the water to see where her mother had gone. She waited a few minutes before she settled in her mind that her mother had finally drowned. Trying to make her way up the embankment that was still slathered with slippery mud, Mary knew that when she reached the top of the embankment, she would report the accident to the authorities. She knew that she would report it in such a way that left out the reality of what had truly happened. Mary dug her fingers deep into the wet mud, trying to reach the top of the embankment. Confident of what she would report, she heard a voice that came out of seemingly nowhere.

"Hey Mary," said a clean-shaven, well-built man with a shaved head.

"Wilson? Is that you?" Mary asked in an overly inquisitive tone.

Wilson responded with an air of nonchalance in his voice, "I'm surprised you recognized me with my new look."

"I would recognize you anywhere, you piece of shit!" Mary responded, anger in her voice and narrowed brows on her face.

"You've been busy since I've been gone," Wilson replied to Mary's hostility. Then, with a sly smile and a grin that stretched menacingly from ear to ear, he added, "Killing all your classmates and even your own mother! Wow, Mary, you must have really hated her to go to such great lengths."

Mary's smile tightened, and with fury in her voice, she responded, "Why did you kill Rachel? You're a... a sick piece of shit!"

The answer was on the tip of Wilson's tongue. "We had plans, Mary, that when she turned 18 we would run off and get married—that was, of course, until you showed up, Mary. I watched the two of you through my upstairs window. I knew I had lost her to you. I knew I had lost my Rachel, and I knew I couldn't go on without her. She was my one and only true love... my soulmate, Mary. So, then one day, I saw her walking to your house to go swimming. That was when I tricked her to go up into the attic to get art supplies. So, I did it—I hit her in the head with a piece of pipe. But somehow, she didn't die; she was still alive. So I took off my belt, wrapped it around her neck, and pulled it tight until she stopped breathing. Then afterward, I moved her downstairs, but I happened to see you and Elizabeth go into the house, so I had to do something. I dragged her through the yard and over to the pool, where I tossed her in. Everyone knows you're a little hot-headed troublemaker, Mary. So now, Mary, you little Jezebel, I really have no choice but to kill you too, and I plan on doing it the same way I killed Rachel."

As Wilson finished telling Mary his secret, he began to slide down the muddy embankment. Smiling, he gave Mary a little wink. "I'm really going to enjoy this, Mary!" he shouted.

Mary stepped back toward the shoreline, smiled, and locked eyes with Wilson.

"What in the world are you smiling about, you crazy girl? You're about to die, and you're smiling?" Wilson asked Mary.

Mary replied, "I'm just really happy right now. I've been waiting and planning for this precise moment for the longest time."

Wilson chuckled. "So, what's your plan? Are you going to kick me between the legs and then claw me to death?"

Mary chuckled back and then asked Wilson, "Have you ever flown before?"

Wilson continued to stare at Mary, his forehead wrinkling in confusion as he replied, "No… why?"

Now, as the only one chuckling, Mary responded in a remarkably confident manner, "Because I'm getting ready to send you to the moon."

Wilson was confused by Mary's candor and inquired, "How are you planning to do that?" As he asked, he reached for his waistline and removed his belt—the same one that had unmercifully taken Rachel's life.

Darkness filled the air, and Mary's eyes darkened as well. Wilson's pants, no longer held up by his belt, fell to the ground. There stood Wilson with his pants around his ankles, wearing a pair of unmistakable boxers imprinted with a ridiculous hearts-and-flowers pattern.

With a glance, Mary lifted Wilson into the sky, similar to how she'd lifted the bus, until he disappeared from sight. Mary smiled and let Wilson plummet from the heavens back toward the calm lake.

CHAPTER TWENTY

Mary continued looking out over the splashdown site when, all of a sudden, a fireball crashed into Wilson's falling pair of pants.

"You've got to be more careful, Mary," Aunt Grace said.

Mary was clearly startled and quickly snapped her head in Grace's direction. "OMG, Aunt Grace... it's YOU!"

To which Grace responded to her niece, "I've been watching this go on for some time now."

Mary asked with confusion and surprise, "Where have you been this whole time?"

"I've been in suspended animation for the last twelve years, waiting for you to grow up and develop your powers," Grace responded.

Grace continued, "So, Mary, did you like what I did to your mother and my stepsister?"

"Wait... what did you do?" Mary was inquisitive.

Grace simply responded, "I drowned her for you."

The final moments before Nacole slipped below the water's surface started to make sense to Mary. "So, you were the one who grabbed her and pulled her down into a watery grave?"

Grace replied in a menacing tone, "Yep, that was me. I didn't want her around anymore. Your mom was very powerful, but she chose not to use her powers. So now, Mary, it's up to you and me, kid."

Mary was confused after hearing this revelation. "Aunt Grace, I never knew my mom had any special powers. I didn't know she was like us. I never once saw her use her powers, so how could I ever know?"

"Mary, she never wanted you to know. She kept her powers to herself—it was her secret that very few knew about. After she found out I was her half-sister, she started to experiment, just like you've been doing. Mary, I had to kill her. Now, once again, it's just us, kid, just you and me." Mary was overwhelmed with emotions and began to cry quietly.

"What's wrong?" Grace inquired as she saw the emotions spilling out of Mary.

"Aunt Grace, I miss my best friend, Rachel. We were best friends, and I loved her so much. We were going to run off together when we both turned eighteen. But when tragedy struck… it really broke my heart, and she was murdered by our neighbor."

Grace snickered and asked, "Was that the guy you shot to the moon and then burned up his pants?"

Mary's tears disappeared, and a slight smile adorned her face as she replied, "Yep... that was him."

Mary continued telling Grace about Rachel. "We had her wake a couple of days ago. I got upset seeing her lying downstairs in that coffin alone... by herself. Aunt Grace, I got so pissed off, I caused a slight tremor. I just wanted her to be left alone. So I slammed her coffin shut and locked it so that no one could bother her again. I sealed her away from the world."

Grace couldn't help but ask a follow-up question. "How long ago did you lock and seal her casket?"

Mary replied, not quite understanding why her aunt was asking, "A couple of days ago. Why?"

Grace then asked another question, further confusing Mary. "So, her casket was locked and sealed but never put in the ground?"

As Mary heard Grace's question, the only response she could give was, "Right," but she still didn't understand where this conversation was going or the reasoning behind it.

Grace helped her understand. "Mary, ever since I was in suspended animation, I've been able to work on and perfect my powers, making them stronger."

"Mmm, I still don't get it, Aunt Grace. Why does it matter?" Mary replied.

Grace put her finger to her lips in a way that said, "Shhh… quiet, child." Grace and Mary locked eyes, and Grace said, "Well, if she's never been buried, then…"

"Then what?" Mary responded, very excited.

Grace calmly continued, "… then I think I can bring her back."

Mary gave a little shriek, followed by a scream full of hope. "Aunt Grace, are you kidding me right now?" She hugged her tightly, saying, "I love you so much, Aunt Grace. I can hardly believe this is possible!"

After creating a little space between them, just enough to breathe, Grace said, "I can't promise anything. I might be able to bring her back if it hasn't been too long."

Mary understood completely and said to her aunt, "Hey, if there's even a chance, I'll take it!" Mary knew that even the slightest chance of getting Rachel back was worth the effort.

Grace smiled and asked, "So, Mary, where is this friend of yours?"

"She's at the church in town, Aunt Grace," Mary replied.

"Okay, but I thought you shook that place down to the ground in the quake, Mary?" Grace asked inquisitively.

Mary giggled at her aunt's comment, grinning. "No, I just gave it a good rattle."

As the conversation moved on, Grace asked, "So, Mary, what does your dad Jimmy look like these days?"

"Oh, blonde hair, blue eyes. Why do you ask?"

Grace simply grinned and asked, "What do you think my chances are if I ask him out on a date?"

Mary laughed and replied to the unexpected question, "I don't really know, to be honest with you, Aunt Grace. Dad likes blondes with big tits, and you're a redhead with medium tits, soooo… it might work."

Mary continued the conversation. "So, Aunt Grace, not to change the subject or anything, but when are you going to teach me how to throw wicked fireballs?"

Grace chuckled and responded, "As soon as you teach me how to launch a person into space."

BETRAYED—KEITH WOLFE

www.ingramcontent.com/pod-product-compliance
Lightning Source LLC
Chambersburg PA
CBHW070645100726
47907CB00007B/2105